DRAGNET

Johnny Fortune meets Ava Gray at the races, and learns that her sister Gail has become involved with a crooked bookmaker, Harvey Chandos. When Johnny helps her to bring Gail home, he's soon up against Nugent, a giant of a man, and Madame Popocopolis, the brain behind Chandos. Popocopolis's plan, to kidnap millionaire's son Roy Belknap for ransom money, is thwarted when she finds herself at the centre of a police dragnet — wanted for murder . . .

CUSTOMER SERVICE EXCELLENCE   **Libraries & Archives**

Kent
County
Council

00884\DTP\RN\07.07   LIB 7

SYDNEY J. BOUNDS

DRAGNET

Complete and Unabridged

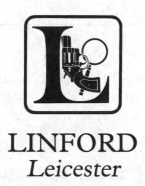

LINFORD
Leicester

First published in Great Britain

First Linford Edition
published 2008

The moral right of the author
has been asserted

British Library CIP Data

Bounds, Sydney J.
　　Dragnet.—Large print ed.—
　　Linford mystery library
　　1. Organized crime—Fiction
　　2. Detective and mystery stories
　　3. Large type books
　　I. Title
　　823.9′14 [F]

　　ISBN 978–1–84782–332–8

Published by
F. A. Thorpe (Publishing)
Anstey, Leicestershire

Set by Words & Graphics Ltd.
Anstey, Leicestershire
Printed and bound in Great Britain by
T. J. International Ltd., Padstow, Cornwall

This book is printed on acid-free paper

1

'I wouldn't bet on *Pegasus*,' said Johnny Fortune.

The girl turned to look at him, her eyes opening wide. She didn't reply, but looked at him carefully, as if trying to make up her mind about something.

'A little bird whispered in my ear,' Johnny said. He lowered his voice. 'The race is fixed. The favourite doesn't have a chance. Try *Rover Boy*.'

The girl blinked her eyes as if she had difficulty in understanding. She drew herself up, and said:

'I don't gamble. I never bet on horses.'

Her voice was as lovely as the rest of her. Johnny felt he could go on listening to her for the rest of his life.

'Never?' he asked lightly. 'You're here to watch the races? You like horses?'

She laughed.

'Is that so strange?' She grew serious. 'But I'm not here to see the races. I'm looking for a man.'

Johnny Fortune smiled happily.

'And now,' he said, 'you've found one.'

The girl shook her head.

'I'm looking for one particular man,' she explained. 'A bookmaker.'

It was Johnny's turn to widen his eyes.

'Why,' he asked, 'is a beautiful young girl, who admits she is not at the track to watch the horses, and never bets, looking for a bookmaker?'

Her face clouded with a mixture of sorrow and anxiety, but persisted in remaining beautiful. Johnny was entranced and intrigued.

'The man I'm looking for is Harvey Chandos. All I know about him is that he's a bookmaker. I wonder, can you point him out to me?'

Johnny frowned. He studied the girl carefully. She was about twenty-three, simply dressed in a flowered cotton frock that showed off her perfect figure. Her hair was a waterfall of bronze, glinting in the bright sunlight, smelling faintly of a delicate perfume. Her face was a smooth oval, with lips lightly caressed with carmine, and wide soft brown eyes flecked with gold.

But it wasn't her striking beauty that affected Johnny, so much as her vibrant character. She was so obviously innocent to the ways of the world, that he wanted to protect her.

'Chandos,' Johnny Fortune said carefully, 'is not a nice man. I'd advise you to leave him alone. I'd advise that very strongly.'

'I have to see him,' she replied. 'It's most important.'

'Hmm,' said Johnny, deliberating. 'Then I'd better go with you. Suppose you tell me why you want to see him.'

'Why should I? It's none of your business and — '

'Quiet!' Johnny snapped, his attention fixed on the horses lining up at the starting post. He brought up his field glasses and studied the horses. The starter's pistol cracked and a shout went up:

'They're off!'

Eleven horses thundered down the straight, past the stand. Johnny, swivelling his glasses, watched them take the bend.

'*Pegasus, Nitelite, Rover Boy* — come on, *Rover Boy!*'

A cloud of dust obscured the leaders as they rounded the corner. Further along the track, people were shouting, cheering on their own favourites. New York's Belmont Park race track was crowded with sporting fans, men with field glasses and flushed faces, women in summer frocks and wide-brimmed hats. Bookies tic-tacked and a radio commentator garbled into his microphone.

The horses were strung out down the far straight, the two leaders ahead by several lengths.

Johnny muttered: '*Pegasus* — and *Rover Boy.*'

The girl beside him asked politely: 'Have you a bet on this race?'

Johnny didn't take his eyes off the horses as they came round the last bend, into the finishing straight. One furlong to go.

'Two hundred bucks on Rover Boy,' he said briefly.

The shouting rose to a deafening roar,

then faded as *Pegasus*, the favourite, began to drop back. It was immediately obvious that *Rover Boy* had a clear field — no other horse was near enough to catch him. Johnny lowered his glasses, grinning as *Rover Boy* cantered past the winning post, with *Pegasus* five lengths behind.

'I'm glad you won,' the girl said. 'Even though I disapprove of gambling.'

'It was a cinch. I had the tip *Pegasus* would be fixed — and now there's a slight matter of eight hundred bucks to collect.'

'Do you mean,' she asked, 'that the race was — crooked?'

Johnny grinned.

'That's the size of it — and you know who fixed it? Your friend, Chandos. *Pegasus* was heavily backed. If the favourite had won, Chandos would have lost a packet — and he isn't the sort to take chances. So *Pegasus* was fixed.'

The girl said, quickly: 'He's no friend of mine.' Curiosity got the better of her. 'How was it done? I mean, how could anyone be sure the horse wouldn't win?'

Johnny Fortune shrugged.

'There's ways,' he said. 'The jockey may be paid to hold back his horse at a critical moment. Or the horse may be doped, so that it will lose stamina over a long distance. Or the horse selected to win may be doped the other way — give it a shot to increase its vitality, stimulate it.'

The girl shuddered.

'That's horrible.'

Johnny nodded grimly.

'Horses that have been doped don't last long.'

'If you knew, why didn't you go to the police?' she challenged.

'It isn't as simple as that. Doping is difficult to detect — and you can bet Chandos wouldn't be directly implicated. He keeps a disbarred jockey for that work — a man who knows just how to dope a horse to get a certain effect. In a way, it's quite a delicate operation requiring a skilled technique and intimate knowledge of horses. And Snowy wouldn't let himself be caught on the job.'

He returned to a previous question.

'Why do you want to see Chandos?'

The girl looked at him closely, weighing

6

him up. She saw a slim young man with a lithe, athletic figure — his grey suit was perfectly cut and obviously expensive. His face was handsome in a casual, debonair manner and his light blue eyes were boldly inviting. His dark hair was sleek and moustache neatly trimmed.

There was undeniable strength of character in his face, and in his strong, tapered hands as he played with a swagger cane. She felt that he was a man she could trust.

'My name is Ava Gray,' she said. 'My sister, Gail, has become involved with Harvey Chandos. I want to see her, to get her away from him.'

Johnny didn't say anything. His face was grave and he shook his head slightly, as if commenting to himself.

Ava Gray went on: 'Gail is younger than me, only nineteen, but she's reckless and headstrong, wanting excitement at any price. We lived together, after father died — Gail's birth took mother from us — in Salisbury, Maryland. But Gail tired of small town life; she left me a year ago, to work in New York as a photographer's model. Her letters became more and more infrequent and I was worried about her. I learnt she had formed an alliance with Harvey Chandos and — well, I want to take her home again. She's young, and needs someone to straighten her out.'

'That's going to be difficult,' Johnny said slowly. 'I know Chandos's reputation. If he is interested in your sister, you're walking into bad trouble. He doesn't give up the things he wants without a fight — and he fights dirty. Anyway, maybe your sister won't want to go back. She may be — '

'I'm sure I can make her see reason, if only I can talk to her, Mr. — er — ?'

'Fortune, Johnny Fortune. My enemies call me Fortune, my friends, Johnny. I hope you'll call me Johnny.'

Ava smiled.

'Very well — Johnny. And now, will you show me Harvey Chandos?'

He sighed.

'Okay. If you're set on it — but I'm coming along. You'll need someone to look after you if you're going against Chandos.'

She regarded him thoughtfully with her wide brown eyes. The gold flecks swirled mysteriously in their depths and she smiled.

'All right,' she said. 'Perhaps I'll need someone to protect me from you — after all, you're a perfect stranger. But I can't stop you coming with me, can I?'

Johnny swung his cane airily. His blue eyes danced with delight.

'You bet you can't,' he said determinedly. He caught her arm and piloted her through the crowd. 'First,' he said, 'we'll stop and collect my winnings — then I'll be able to stand you dinner tonight.'

Ava laughed softly.

'You're a very persuasive young man — perhaps I shan't be hungry.'

Johnny winked and pressed her hand.

'Beware of the wolf,' he said mockingly. 'So many lovely young girls have fallen for my persuasive ways. You're only one of a very long list!'

She looked away.

'I think I can trust you. I like you — Johnny.'

He scowled villainously and struck a pose.

'Pah! Foiled — how can I lure you to my apartment if you put me on my honour?'

'I thought villains didn't have any honour?'

'This one has — unfortunately!'

He laughed delightedly at the pun. She said, laughingly,

'I shall regard you as my chaperon in this city of vice.'

They reached the bookmaker's enclosure. Johnny found his bookie and handed in his winning ticket.

'You're too lucky, Fortune,' the man said, paying over his eight hundred in winnings. 'You'll break me if you carry on winning.'

Johnny grinned, tucking the money in his wallet.

'Just making my fortune! See you later, Bill . . .'

Bill looked at Ava and raised his eyebrows.

'I guess that won't last you long,' he said. 'Not with mink the price it is!'

Two girls rushed up, ignoring Ava. They threw their arms round Johnny's neck and kissed him, one on each cheek.

'Oh, Johnny — how nice to see you . . . '

'Johnny — darling!'

Johnny Fortune disengaged himself with a graceful movement.

'Hello, Vi. Hello, Jill. Nice to see you girls again.'

'We didn't know you were back in town, Johnny. Where have you been? Going to the Orchid Club tonight? Say, Johnny, if you don't have a date . . . '

Johnny took a firmer hold on Ava Gray's arm, smiling gently.

'Open your gorgeous eyes, girls, and you'll see I'm not likely to be free for some time. Now, if you'll excuse us, we have a little business to attend to.'

Both girls looked at Ava, smiling; they didn't seem at all surprised that Johnny was escorting a new girlfriend. They winked, chanted a cheery 'See you sometime, Johnny,' and merged into the crowd.

Ava said: 'Perhaps I should have taken

your wolf character more seriously?' But she was laughing.

Johnny grinned

'I can't say I've ever been lonely — but right now, there's only one girl in my life.'

He looked steadily at Ava, and his light tone had an undercurrent of seriousness. She looked away, blushing slightly. Johnny Fortune was the sort of man girls run after and, if he preferred her company, well that was a nice compliment. Ava's heart beat a little quicker as she realized this.

Johnny was pushing his way through the crowd. He put gentle pressure on Ava's hand, and murmured:

'Harvey Chandos.'

Ava looked at the man her sister was mixed up with. She saw a heavily built man who was beginning to put on fat round the waistline. His blotched, reddish face and the dark bags under his eyes told her he must be past forty, that he hadn't lived a particularly healthy life. His eyes were cold and hard, giving the impression of a man used to taking what he wanted by force and giving nothing of himself in return. His suit and the jeweled rings on his fingers told her he had plenty of money. Ava felt repelled by him, and wondered what her sister could see in Harvey Chandos.

The bookmaker was talking to a small, stunted man with a shock of hair and wild eyes. He was curiously dressed in a well-cut drape suit, the effect spoiled by a cheap striped shirt and checkered cloth cap. His lean face had a nervous twitch to it and the hard outline of a gun showed under his left armpit. Johnny recognized the eyes of a dope-taker.

Both men stopped talking as Johnny piloted Ava towards them. Chandos said:

'Why, Gail, I thought — '

He broke off, looking closer at Ava Gray, his face showing a puzzled expression. Johnny grinned.

'Hello Chandos. This is Miss Ava Gray, Gail's sister, which accounts for your mistake. Hi, Snowy, how's the fixing racket these days?'

Snowy, the stunted man with the shock of hair, stared bleak-eyed at Johnny Fortune. His voice was soft and threatening:

'You talk too much, Fortune.'

Chandos had recovered his aplomb. He knew he'd given himself away in confusing Ava with Gail, that it was no use denying he knew Gail Gray. He took a fat cigar from an aluminium tube, pierced the end and lit up with a flourish.

'Nice to meet you, Miss Gray,' he said smoothly. 'Staying long in New York? Pity your sister's out of town — she'd have liked to meet you, I know. Can I take a message?'

Ava said: 'I'm staying till I see my sister, Mr. Chandos. Will you please tell me where I can find her? I want to talk to her.'

The smile faded from Harvey Chandos's face. His voice became clipped, cold.

'I'd advise you to go home. Gail doesn't want to see you. Better see her off on the next train, Fortune.'

He turned away, moved across to a sleek, high-powered Airflow. Snowy said: 'Yeah, send her home, Fortune.' He, too, crossed to the car. Chandos drove off without looking back.

Ava frowned, but her face, Johnny observed, persisted in remaining beautiful. He'd never met a girl who could do that before.

'I won't be treated like that,' Ava said decisively. 'I shall insist on talking to my sister — I won't let her stay another minute with that horrible man!'

Johnny looked grave. It was his opinion that Ava was headed for trouble if she tried to take Gail away from Harvey Chandos.

He said: 'Maybe it would be best if you went home. If Gail is mixed up with Chandos, she's in deep. I doubt there's anything you can do to change matters.'

Ava was angry.

'You don't seem to think much of my sister, Mr. Fortune. She's a nice girl, just a little wild, that's all. I'm sure I can make her see reason if only I can talk with her alone.'

Her expression softened.

'I'm sorry, Johnny, I know you're trying to help — but I won't leave New York without Gail. Will you help me find her?'

Johnny stared into soft brown eyes and

saw calm resolution. He sighed.

'All right, Ava. I guess you'd go ahead on your own anyway, so I'll help you. But don't underestimate Chandos — he's a nasty piece of work.' He hesitated, then added: 'He won't stop at murder if he thinks you can make trouble for him.'

Ava Gray shuddered.

'Poor Gail. I can't let her down now. I must save her.'

Johnny pressed her arm.

'All right, we'll do what we can. Now, how about that dinner date? If I'm crossing swords with Harvey Chandos, I feel the need for a little alcoholic refreshment first!'

2

A grey, low-slung coupé drew up outside the *Dutch Oven*. Johnny Fortune helped Ava Gray out of the car and took her arm as they went into the restaurant on Springfield Boulevard in Queens Village.

The doorman said: 'Hi, Johnny,' and turned to call to the man behind the counter: 'Johnny Fortune's back again.'

Dutch Evans hastened up, bald head gleaming, eyes sparkling. He was a short, plump man with a white apron and chef's tall hat. He grabbed Johnny's hand and pumped vigorously.

'Glad to see you, Johnny.' He took time off to look at Ava, and with an obvious effort of self-control refrained from whistling. 'You sure pick 'em, Johnny. Glad to meet you, miss, and any friend of Johnny's is a friend of mine.'

Ava smiled, basking in the warmth of Dutch Evans' affection for Johnny. She murmured a polite, 'Thanks.'

Johnny said: 'A quiet table in the corner where we can talk.'

'Sure, Johnny, I know.' Dutch winked at the girl. 'I'll fix two specials. And you'll dance while you're waiting, miss? Best floor in New York State. Best food in the country!'

He hurried away to the kitchen to superintend personally the cooking of two specials. Johnny led Ava between the tables, to the parquet strip serving as dance floor. Music came from a juke box.

Johnny, guiding Ava into a quick-step, said:

'I hope you don't mind? I know we've a lot to talk about but Dutch is a good friend — he'd be hurt if we didn't have one dance. And he does cook the best food in New York.'

She smiled.

'I'm enjoying it, Johnny. You're a good dancer.' She added: 'Do you bring all your girlfriends here? You seem very well known — and liked.'

He laughed softly.

'I've three diaries full of telephone numbers. Remind me to show you after

18

you've looked at my etchings!'

The record finished and Johnny took her to a corner table screened by curtains. The lighting was soft and discreet, the atmosphere intimate. It was early in the evening and the *Dutch Oven* almost empty, so they could talk without lowering their voices.

'Do you know where Harvey Chandos lives?' Ava asked.

'No, but I can find out. I've a friend at police headquarters. You weren't thinking of visiting him?'

She nodded.

'Of course. I must see Gail as soon as possible.'

Johnny looked at Ava's lovely face, her bronze hair and soft brown eyes. He thought it would be a pity if all that beauty was spoiled. He said, firmly:

'I can't allow that — it would be dangerous. I'll find out where Chandos lives and call myself. I'll arrange for her to meet you somewhere. How does that sound?'

'She's my sister,' Ava said quietly. 'I'll go myself.'

Johnny shook his head vigorously. His debonair manner quite deserted him and his light blue eyes went cold.

'No, Ava, we'll do it my way. I can handle Chandos — I'm used to tough guys like him. And I can fix the meeting for tomorrow. You can wait till then, can't you?'

She hesitated, looking him straight in the face.

'If it's as dangerous as you say, Johnny, I can't ask you to do my duty. There's no reason for you to become involved — '

He held her hand a moment.

'There's a good reason,' he said, 'and you don't need me to tell you what that is. I never felt about anyone the way I do about you.'

She lowered her eyes, murmured:

'All right, Johnny, we'll do it your way.'

He smiled happily and the grimness left him. He stood up, said:

'I'll make a 'phone call. Shan't be long.'

Johnny Fortune crossed the floor to the 'phone booth and inserted a coin in the slot. He dialled a number and listened:

'Police Headquarters, New York City.'

Johnny said: 'I want to speak to Lieutenant Dix, Homicide.'

There was a pause, then:

'Lieutenant Dix speaking. Who's that?'

Dix had a silky voice, rather high-pitched.

'This is Johnny Fortune, Dix. I want Harvey Chandos's address. Can you get it for me?'

'Sure. Hold the line, Johnny.'

Dix's voice, muffled, shouted at some-one in headquarters. He used the telephone again:

'Didn't know you were in town, Johnny. What's cooking with Chandos? He run off with your girl? Or forgot to pay your winnings?'

Johnny said: 'I don't bet with Chandos — and no one runs off with any date of mine. What d'you know about Gail Gray? I believe she's mixed up with Chandos.'

Dix said: 'Quite a looker, but I wouldn't want her for my daughter. I'd put her across my knee and spank the life outa her. She's spoilt — runs around with any man who has enough money to give her a good time. Chandos is the latest on her list. I guess she'll come to a bad end — and not so far in the future at that. What's your angle on her?'

'Nothing yet. Just collecting information. What happened to that address you were getting?'

Johnny heard the rustle of paper, a murmur of voices, then Dix said:

'Chandos lives at 7566a Myrtle Avenue, overlooking Cypress Hills Cemetery, in Glendale. You wouldn't be gunning for him, huh?'

'Me, lieutenant? You know I never carry a gun!'

Johnny replaced the telephone and looked at it thoughtfully. Ava was going to get a shock when she found out the way Gail had been living in New York.

Well, there was nothing he could do about that. He left the 'phone booth and went back to their table, arriving as Dutch Evans brought the specials.

'Steak with mushrooms and all the trimmings,' Dutch beamed.

'Fine,' Johnny said. 'Let's eat.'

Dutch went away, and Ava asked, eagerly: 'Did you find out?'

Johnny nodded, cutting himself a slice of steak and heaping mushrooms on his fork.

'But I'm keeping it to myself — I don't want you running over there and getting into trouble as soon as my back's turned. Tell me some more about Gail.'

Ava began eating too. She said:

'We're very alike to look at, though we're not twins — that's how Chandos made his mistake. She's young and impetuous, thinks a lot of clothes and having a good time, but there's no real harm in her. She had a job as photographer's model before she met Chandos. I'm sure he must have some hold over her.'

'Maybe Chandos hasn't been the only one,' Johnny said. 'How did she behave at home?'

'She had a lot of boyfriends, of course; she's very beautiful, but I'm sure she never did anything wrong. Since Dad died, she became restless; small-town life wasn't exciting enough for her. That's why she came to New York . . . I'm sure Chandos must have forced her into this horrible situation.'

Johnny wasn't feeling so sure about that. He'd seen young, excitable girls before; usually, they found out too late that there are more important things in life than spending money recklessly and having a good time with any man rich enough to buy them mink and nylon.

He said: 'A year's a long time. She may have changed a lot, Ava. Best not to expect too much when you see her.'

Ava Gray looked at her plate. She asked, slowly:

'You think she's — bad?'

Johnny shrugged. He repeated:

'A year's a long time. A person can change.'

Dutch waddled up, smiling.

'Good, huh? What you want now? Fruit Melba with coffee?'

Ava nodded. Johnny corrected;

' . . . with rye!'

Fresh fruit, cherries, peach, pear and apricots were covered with a cone of whipped cream. Johnny finished his rye and lit a cigarette; Ava didn't smoke.

Johnny asked: 'Where are you staying?

I'll put you in a cab and see you off before I visit Chandos.'

Ava replied: 'Courtfield Hotel on East 43rd Street, near the Grand Central Terminal. You'll 'phone me as soon as you leave Chandos's place?'

'Alternatively,' Johnny said carelessly, 'you could wait at my apartment. I've some pleasant etchings . . . '

'All right, Johnny.' She laughed. 'To prove that I trust you, I will.'

They left the *Dutch Oven* and Johnny gave her the key to his apartment. He called a cab and instructed the driver:

'Java Buildings, Vernon Boulevard, Long Island City.'

The cab moved off. Johnny Fortune watched it out of sight, then turned away. He hoped Ava wasn't going to be badly hurt over this business, but he was afraid she was. He sighed; he'd have done anything to protect her from her sister's folly.

He got behind the wheel of his grey coupé and drove off. It was a little after eight in the evening and the sun was going down; the summer air was still warm, with a cooling breeze blowing wisps of high cloud across the sky. He left Springfield and headed down Hillside Avenue, travelling west. He drove, without hurry, through Hollis and Jamaica, thinking how quiet Queens was compared with Manhattan; here were none of the bustling crowds, the bright lights and flashing neon signs of Broadway.

It was a peaceful residential area with concrete blocks of flats interspersed with brownstone houses and spacious gardens. New Yorkers sauntered rather than hurried to their evening's rendezvous. Johnny turned diagonal right at Metropolitan Avenue, to cross Forest Park and pick up the Union Turnpike. He followed the boundary of the park to Myrtle Avenue and Cypress Hills Cemetery. 7566a was across the road from the cemetery, a white-walled edifice of concrete in the modern style, with ten stories, a penthouse, and rows of wide, sun-trap windows.

Johnny parked the coupé and went through swing doors to the foyer. There were no names on the call button panel, just numbers. The system was very discreet. He found a bell-boy and asked:

'What floor for Harvey Chandos?'

'Penthouse. What name shall I say?'

Johnny Fortune smiled as he passed the bell-boy a ten-spot.

'I'm an old friend of Harvey. I'd like to surprise him.'

'Sure, I get it,' said the bell-boy, tucking the note away. 'I ain't seen yuh, mister. The elevator's over by the palms.'

The elevator was self-operating, Johnny started up, pressing the penthouse 'stop' button. The cage was silent, smooth, and fast. It stopped, and Johnny operated the door, stepping out to find himself in a roof garden. Chandos's apartment was roofed with a glass dome and most of the walls were glass. Harvey seemed to like sunlight.

He pressed the bell-push and waited, swinging his cane. The door opened and Johnny saw the wild eyes and shock of hair belonging to Snowy. He leaned on the door, forcing it wide open, pushing past the disbarred jockey.

'I'm looking for Gail Gray,' he drawled,

staring into the room.

It was a large room with plenty of light. The floor was completely covered by a thick pile decorated with tigers; it must have cost several thousand dollars and the room was furnished in the same expensive style.

There were four persons in the room, not counting Snowy.

The girl who looked like Ava, turned her head and looked carelessly at Johnny. She said:

'I don't think I know you.'

Johnny moved towards her, using his eyes. She was almost the twin of Ava Gray, with the same beautiful figure and bronze hair. Her eyes were brown and flecked with gold, but there was no softness to them; they were the eyes of a girl who had been asked all the questions and had learnt the answers the hard way.

She was dressed in a maroon-coloured evening dress with bare shoulders and smoked a cigarette through a long-stemmed holder of black jade. If Johnny hadn't known she was only nineteen, he'd have thought her several years older than

Ava. The bloom of youth had worn off and she used a lot of make-up to hide the fact.

Chandos watched Johnny over the glowing tip of his cigar. The bookmaker was uneasy, wary. He said:

'What do you want, Fortune?'

Snowy, coming up behind Johnny, grunted:

'He forced his way in, Chan. I couldn't stop him.'

Johnny smiled coldly.

'That's right, Chandos,' he drawled. 'I'm a hard person to stop. Right now, I want to talk with Gail Gray — I thought you might have forgotten to mention her sister was in town.'

'Ava?' Gail sounded surprised and a little uneasy. Johnny guessed she would be ashamed to meet her sister, face to face.

His eyes moved past Chandos to the giant negro. He was over seven feet high and broad to match, with tiny eyes, bright as pinpoints. He was brightly dressed in green gaberdine slacks and a flashy, check sports coat, open to show a crimson shirt and hand-painted tie featuring a nude blonde. His brown shoes were soled with inch-thick crepe and his frizzy hair was uncovered.

'Yo wan' me to take him, Chan?' the giant said, moving silently forward, clenching massive dark-skinned hands. He looked happy at the thought.

'Not now, Nugent,' Harvey Chandos said. 'Gail can deal with Fortune, tell him he's not wanted round these parts. We don't want trouble.'

He pronounced the giant's name, 'Noo — gent.' The giant relaxed and Johnny could see his muscles ripple under his clothes.

Nugent said, grumbling: 'That sho is a pity, Chan.'

Johnny ignored Nugent and concentrated all his attention on the fourth person in the room. Nugent and Snowy were small-time; Gail an empty-headed girl who used her body to get what she wanted; Chandos was hard, a man who would kill if necessary; but it was the ugly old woman who impressed him most.

He'd heard of Madame Popocopolis,

but he'd never met her before. Few people had — or wanted to. Rumour said she was the brain behind Chandos, that he took orders from her, and, looking at her, Johnny found that easy to believe.

She must have been over sixty and took no trouble to hide her years. She was fatter than any woman Johnny had ever seen; her whole body, clad in a soiled dress of black velvet, was composed of roll upon roll of fat. Her enormous bosom sagged and her stomach bulged, her legs and arms were short and barrel-like. Her face was almost beautifully ugly and would have fascinated an artist.

Piggy eyes peered under bushy eyebrows and her double chins merged without break into a thick, dirty grey neck. Her hair was grey, thinning into an unkempt straggle. Her very fatness was crinkled in lines of age and dissipation. But her eyes were bright with cunning and criminal intelligence, eyes that coldly calculated the menace in Johnny as they watched each other. Her voice, when she spoke, was remarkably firm, as if she formed each syllable separately and used it deliberately.

'So you're Johnny Fortune? I've heard a lot about you, young man. I've heard that you're daring and resourceful, that you never consider the odds against you; well, this time, I'd advise you to think carefully before attempting to pit your strength and brains against me. I shan't warn you again young man — I shall crush you utterly. Gail, tell Johnny Fortune how much you want to see your sister.'

Johnny felt a cold shiver run down his spine. There was something frightening about Madame Popocopolis, like a spider in its web, spinning threads of doom. Gail Gray shot the old woman a look of hatred; probably she hated her power over Harvey Chandos. Perhaps Madame Popocopolis was jealous of Gail's beauty, too. There was no doubt of the feeling of hatred between the two women.

Gail poured herself a slug of gin; she took a half-pint tumbler and drank it, hardly noticing. She lit a fresh cigarette and said:

'You can tell Ava I never want to see her again. Tell her to leave me alone. I'm tired of her stuck-up ways. She's a prude, a spoilsport, and I'm not going to let her interfere with my life. Tell her to go back to Salisbury and forget about me. Is that plain enough?'

She laughed, a harsh, jeering sound that made Johnny sorry for her — and Ava. Ava wasn't going to like the change in her sister. He said:

'Yeah, that's plain enough,' and left.

3

Madame Popocopolis watched Johnny Fortune leave, then turned her piggy eyes on Gail Gray. She said:

'Does your sister know about Roy Belknap?'

Harvey Chandos scowled at the girl, champing on his cigar.

'It's going to put us on the spot if she does,' he grunted.

Gail laughed.

'You're a fine bunch of crooks,' she jeered. 'Scared of your own shadows. Of course Ava doesn't know — you think I run around telling that innocent little prude everything I do?'

Chandos's breath came out with a little sigh; there were beads of sweat on his forehead.

'That's all right then. Nothing to worry about — except Johnny Fortune!'

Madame Popocopolis moved in her chair. Her double chins shook as a cackle of laughter came from her thick lips. It was a sound that made Gail shudder.

'We'll go ahead with our plan for tonight,' Madame Popocopolis said firmly. 'If Johnny Fortune interferes, you'll kill him. We cannot afford to take half measures with that young man — but I think Gail's sister will go home after Fortune delivers her message. If not, she too must die. The stakes are too big for us to risk discovery.'

Nugent and Snowy said nothing; both of them were afraid of the fat woman. They waited for their orders. Madame Popocopolis shifted her obese bulk again, her eyes boring into the painted mask of Gail Gray's face. She said:

'You know what you've got to do? Repeat your orders.'

Gail flared up angrily.

'I'm not a child — I know the plan for tonight. Can't you leave me alone, you old hag? You're jealous because I'm beautiful, because I can make Harvey do what I want. I know you hate me and — '

The fat woman's voice cracked like a whip.

'You poor child!' Ridicule and contempt rang in her tone, getting under Gail's skin. 'I'm not jealous of your looks. Harvey takes his orders from me, and so do you — never forget that. Harvey's like any other man, he likes a pretty face and a soft young body to play with. Well, that's all right, so long as it doesn't interfere with business.' Her voice hardened. 'But if I give the word, Harvey will kill you!'

Gail shuddered, looking at Chandos for comfort.

He took her in his arms, kissed her lips, caressed her gently.

'Everything's all right, Gail,' he said soothingly. 'No one's going to hurt you — if you do as you're told.'

He stared at Madame Popocopolis and said:

'You shouldn't frighten Gail like that. Remember, she's one of us, now.'

The fat woman cackled with laughter.

'Till you tire of her, Harvey; only till then!' She turned on Gail again.

'I let Harvey have you when I found out you knew Roy Belknap. I knew you'd

36

be useful to us. Now, repeat your orders.'

Gail obeyed, sulkily.

'I telephoned Roy, this afternoon — '

Madame Popocopolis interrupted: 'From where?'

'A public call box. It can't be traced. I told him I wanted to see him again, that I realized I was in love with him, that I was in trouble and needed his help. I made him promise to meet me in secret — '

'Where?'

Gail replied: 'At Goose Creek station, on Rulers Bar Hassock, in Jamaica Bay. I told him to take a single ticket by rail and tell no one where he was going.'

'Good!' Madame Popocopolis purred with satisfaction. She asked: 'Are you sure he'll come?'

Gail laughed.

'Sure I'm sure! The dope's in love with me — why, he even wanted to marry me. Imagine that!'

She laughed again, kissing Chandos casually.

'He'll do what I tell him, all right.'

The fat woman said: 'And when you meet him tonight? What will you do?'

Gail said: 'Take him to the creek where I'll find Nugent and Snowy waiting with the boat.'

'And make sure you're not followed. What time did you say?'

'Eleven o'clock.'

Madame Popocopolis transferred her attention from Gail to Snowy and Nugent.

'You two — what do you do?'

Snowy's face twitched nervously under the direct gaze of the fat woman. He said:

'We have the boat waiting in the creek at ten-forty-five. When Gail shows up with Belknap, we knock him out — '

Nugent's black face gleamed with the pleasure of anticipation. His large hands opened and closed menacingly. He said:

'Ah takes care o' that. Leave him to me. It will sho be a pleasure to get mah hands on Mister Belknap.'

Madame Popocopolis said, sharply: 'You must be careful not to kill him, Nugent. He's no good to us dead. Only hit him hard enough to make him unconscious.'

The giant grinned broadly.

'Sho, ma'am, I not hurt him much.'

Snowy continued: 'We take the boat, with Gail and Belknap to the hut on Silver Bar, where you'll be waiting for us. That'll be about eleven-thirty.'

The fat woman nodded in satisfaction.

'Good. And Harvey — the hut is ready for us? No one has learnt of our preparations?'

Chandos said: 'It's ready. All the arrangements were made in secret — no one knows.'

He paced the room, frowning. Finally, he crushed out his cigar, turned to face Madame Popocopolis and said:

'I don't like it. Kidnapping's a tough racket — not in our line. It's still not too late to change your mind — '

The fat woman said, firmly:

'I'm not changing my mind, Harvey. We're going through with it — this is the chance I've been waiting for and I'm taking it. I'm tired of playing the tracks, making a few thousand bucks and taking risks out of all proportion to the profit. This time we're going to clean up in a big way — then skip across the border.'

Her eyes shone and a cackle of laughter pealed through the room.

'It was a stroke of luck, Gail knowing Roy Belknap, the only son of Thaddeus Belknap, multi-millionaire. He'll pay a fine ransom to get his son back, say about twenty million dollars!'

Gail Gray's brown eyes lit up, the golden flecks in them swirling like sunlight on autumn leaves. Roy Belknap meant nothing to her; he was too strait-laced, too milk-and-water to appeal to her. She didn't care what happened to him — but twenty million bucks!

She'd get her share — and Harvey Chandos too.

★ ★ ★

A nearby church clock chimed nine o'clock as Johnny Fortune reached Long Island City, after leaving the penthouse home of Harvey Chandos. His grey coupé moved along Vernon Boulevard till he came to Java buildings, opposite Rainey Park. He parked the car and went through the foyer, took the elevator to the eighth floor. He buzzed the push-button of his apartment and Ava Gray opened the door.

Johnny went in, light blue eyes smiling, jauntily swinging his cane. Ava looked refreshingly beautiful after her sister; he regarded her with approval.

'Well,' she said, 'did you see Gail? How is she? When can I meet her?'

The questions gushed out, revealing how much Ava cared for her sister, how she longed to see her again. Johnny evaded the questions for the moment; he hadn't quite figured how to break his news to Ava. He poured himself a drink, lit a cigarette, and gestured to the pictures on the walls.

'See, I really have etchings!'

Ava nodded. She'd already admired the character studies by Van Abbé.

'They're artist's proofs, aren't they? You're quite a connoisseur.'

She sat down, crossing her hands on her knees, waiting for him to speak. It was a small, tastefully furnished apartment, completely in character with Johnny himself. He sat opposite her, a lithe, debonair figure.

He said, abruptly: 'I saw your sister at Chandos's. She said she didn't want to see you, that she wanted you to leave her alone. She wants you to go back to Salisbury and forget about her.'

Ava gave a small cry of anguish.

'She didn't mean that?' she pleaded. 'Gail couldn't be so cruel.'

Johnny finished his rye and drew at his cigarette. He placed his hands over Ava's and looked into her eyes trying to keep his voice steady.

'You have to face it, Ava. Gail has changed completely since you saw her last, New York's had a bad effect on her. She's hard, right through to the core, finished with your way of life — '

Ava's hands clenched and she bit her lip. She tossed her head, bronze curls shaking, gold flecks swirling in her soft brown eyes. Her voice was low and desperate.

'I can't believe it — I won't! I must go to her — if I can only talk with her, I'm sure I can — '

Johnny shook his head.

'It's too late for that,' he said flatly. He got up and paced the room. A sudden gleam came into his blue eyes. He said:

'If you like, I'll bring her here — but it won't do any good.'

Ava opened her eyes wide.

'What do you mean?' she asked.

Johnny laughed softly. He was again the gay adventurer, prepared to stake his life to help a lovely girl in trouble.

'I mean,' he murmured, 'that I'll return to Chandos's apartment and kidnap your sister! I'll bring her here whether she wants to come or not — but how you'll keep her from going back to Chandos as soon as your back's turned, I don't know.'

He considered it briefly, added: 'Maybe you can put her under a doctor's care — send her to a private sanatorium. I can't think of any other way.'

Ava shuddered.

'She isn't — I mean — '

'No, she's not insane. Not in the medical sense. But she certainly needs treatment to get this poison out of her system — the poison that's ruined her youth, made her a confirmed gin-drinker, perhaps a dope-taker.'

Ava covered her face. Johnny said:

'Shall I bring her here? Do you want that?'

She nodded, without speaking. Johnny passed her his handkerchief and she wiped her eyes, trying to smile back at him. Johnny's fists clenched; it hurt him to see Ava cry — maybe he'd get tough with Harvey Chandos. It was time somebody taught Chandos that crime doesn't pay.

He moved to the window and drew back the curtain, looking out over New York, at the blaze of light illuminating the night sky. He felt Ava cross the room and stand beside him.

'That's Welfare Island, in the East River,' he told the girl, pointing downward. 'To the left, you can see the Queensboro Bridge; upstream is Hell Gate and Wards Island. Beyond Welfare, you can see Manhattan and the Franklin Roosevelt Drive.'

Ava looked across the river, to the lofty skyscrapers, marvelling at the intricate network of lights that made the city seem like a fairy world. It was a breath-taking sight.

Johnny said, softly: 'It's a great city, and I wouldn't live anywhere else for all the money in the world, but sometimes I get furious, thinking of all the crooks hiding behind those bright lights, ruining honest people's lives for a few filthy dollars. Chandos is only one of them.'

She touched his arm, smiling.

'I like you, Johnny. You're good — and gentle. You'll help Gail, won't you?'

He let the curtain fall back in place, blocking out the view of the night and the city. His arms went round Ava, drew her close. He bent his head, kissed her lips, murmuring:

'Ava, darling, there isn't anything I won't do for you. I'll help Gail — if I can . . . '

Gently, she broke away from him, pulse racing, eyes shining. She moved to a chair and sat down, watching him pour himself another rye. He sipped it thoughtfully, lighting a fresh cigarette.

'Are you what they call — an adventurer?' she asked.

45

'I guess so. Anyway, I like adventure, and thrills and danger. I like helping people in trouble, especially lovely young girls — you might say it's been my hobby, my way of life.'

He blew a smoke ring, smiling at his own thoughts.

'More than one crook has reason to regret meeting Johnny Fortune,' he went on. 'There are some smart operators in town that the police can't touch. I go after them. The cops don't worry what happen to crooks like that and sometimes I get a little unofficial help. Sometimes I'm able to help the police get evidence against a gangster they badly want. You see, I'm outside the law, so I don't have to be particular about my methods. And I take some money off my crook victims at times, enough to live on without working.'

Ava smiled faintly.

'A sort of modern Robin Hood?' she suggested.

He laughed.

'I've been called that before — and other things!'

Ava said, impulsively: 'I'm glad I met you, Johnny. I have a feeling that you're the right person to help Gail, if anyone can.'

Johnny Fortune frowned: 'If anyone can!' The words had an ominous ring to them, as if Gail Gray was already beyond help.

'It's early yet,' he said. 'I'll wait till one o'clock — by then, Gail and Chandos should be alone. I can handle Chandos all right — I'll have Gail out of that penthouse and into my car before he knows what's happened.'

Ava's face was flushed with excitement.

'Tell me about your life,' she said. 'You must have had a lot of thrills.'

He grinned at her.

'Do you want to know about the blonde in Chicago, the redhead on Broadway, or — '

'You're trying to make me jealous,' she accused lightly. 'I don't believe you've ever loved anyone before!'

Johnny made a mock-angry face, like a small boy caught stealing candy.

'That's a slur on my character! How

47

can I play the wolf if you won't take me seriously?'

She laughed softly.

'But I do take you seriously, Johnny. You've lured me to your apartment and I've seen your etchings.' Her eyes twinkled mischievously. 'What happens next?'

Johnny sighed unhappily.

'I guess there's nothing for it,' he replied, 'but to tell you the story of my life!'

Ava listened, fascinated, while Johnny Fortune described some of his adventures; how he had busted powerful gangs and righted wrongs, rescued damsels in distress and avenged murders the police had never solved. The hours passed unnoticed as he told his story. A clock chimed midnight and Johnny finished. He rose, picked up his swagger cane and moved to the door.

'Time to visit friend Chandos,' he grinned, blue eyes gleaming. 'Sit tight, Ava, and I'll bring Gail to see you.'

He went down by the elevator and got behind the wheel of his coupé. The car travelled fast, along 35th to Steinway, cutting down 39th Street to Queens Boulevard. The wide concrete highway was nearly deserted as he sped eastwards towards Glendale, the moon shining pale silver over the houses and apartment blocks.

He turned down Woodhaven and Dry Harbor, passing St. John's Cemetery, with the white gravestones jutting up like gleaming marble fingers. Cooper Avenue and 76th Street brought him opposite 7566a Myrtle Avenue and Harvey Chandos's penthouse. He kept in shadow, avoiding the night clerk's desk and using the self-operated elevator to reach the roof garden.

The penthouse was dark and silent under the moon. Johnny approached the door, listened a moment, then used a piece of thin steel wire to turn the lock. He opened the door and stepped into darkness.

4

Roy Belknap stepped off the train at Goose Creek station and stared the length of the deserted wooden platform. He was the only passenger to alight from the train, the last train that night. The engine whistled, and the single coach pulled out of the station, out over the bridge spanning Jamaica Bay, heading for the terminal at Rockaway Park.

He glanced at his wristwatch; three minutes to eleven. Frowning, he looked for Gail Gray, wondering why she had chosen such a lonely place for this rendezvous, worried at the trouble she had hinted about. He pulled the soft felt hat down over his eye and thrust his hands deep into his pockets of the light-weight raincoat.

Belknap walked to the ticket office, left his ticket on the ledge, for there was no one to collect it at that time of night, and moved through the wooden box-like hall to the road outside. He was a tall young man, with blonde hair and a handsome face; his clothes were expensive and he wore them with the casual air of a man used to the best of everything. His father spoiled him, never kept him short of money.

At twenty-one, Roy Belknap thought he knew about women — and was wrong. He was in love with Gail and thought she loved him — and was wrong again. He'd never had much experience with girls and when Gail had come along, he'd gone overboard for her. And now she was in some sort of trouble, had appealed to him for help. He swelled with pride at the thought, and his hand closed round the case in his raincoat pocket. The case contained a diamond necklace that had cost him twenty thousand dollars, a small sum to a millionaire's son, a trinket to please Gail.

He'd obeyed her instructions exactly, keeping his trip secret; he was still young enough to fancy himself as a knight setting off to rescue a damsel in distress — the idea captured his imagination, making him forget the danger he invited in such a lonely place. Belknap looked round him; the road was a dry mud path running from the creek to the main Cross Bay Boulevard, and there seemed to be no one about.

'Roy — I'm over here.'

He turned, recognizing Gail's voice, seeing the girl hidden in the shadow of the railroad station. He went towards her quickly, caught her in his arms, calling:

'Gail, dearest!'

She let him kiss her, but didn't return his kiss with much enthusiasm. Gail Gray was thinking only of getting Roy out of sight before some chance passer-by saw them together. She pulled at his arm, whispered.

'Follow me — I'll explain presently. We can't talk here. I must get away from this place.'

She put on a good act, the act of a frightened girl needing help desperately, afraid of an enemy lurking in the shadows, Obediently, Roy Belknap followed as she led the way down to the water, along a ridge of rocks and sand.

Their path was hidden from the land by a sheltering wall of rock, and the moon, coming between drifts of cloud, showed enough light for them to see.

'Tell me what's wrong, Gail,' Belknap urged.

'Where are we going?'

'Later,' she replied, hurrying on. 'If you love me, follow — and don't ask questions.'

He said: 'You know I love you, Gail darling. I want to marry you, to look after you. Why don't we go to my father — he's got a lot of power. He can help you, whatever it is.'

'No,' she said sharply. 'This is between the two of us. You and me — you haven't mentioned your coming out here to anyone?'

She tensed, waiting his reply.

'No one,' Belknap swore.

Gail relaxed, smiling in the darkness, confident of her power over him. There would be no trouble; it was going to be easy. They walked on again.

'You're not still angry with me?' Belknap asked in a low voice.

She laughed: 'Of course not. Would I have asked you to meet me if I were?'

He felt better. Their last meeting had ended in a quarrel; he knew there had been other men in her life and it was this that had made him jealous — he'd spoken in haste, bitterly, and Gail had walked out on him. Now, knowing she really cared, he wanted to marry her, to help her. He watched her as the moon showed again; she was so young, so beautiful, a red evening dress showing under her fur wrap. Her bronze hair was uncovered, flowing down over her shoulders, and gold flecks swirled in her brown eyes.

He frowned; she was too young to have had such experience with men. He put the thought from his mind — he wouldn't let his jealousy come between them again. He felt in his pocket, pulled out the case and opened it.

'For you, Gail,' he murmured.

The sparkle of diamonds in the moonlight caught her eye. She stopped, gasping with delight. The necklace fascinated her. She pulled it from the case and held it to the light.

'They're beautiful,' she breathed.

Roy Belknap fastened the necklace about her throat, kissed her again. The empty case dropped to the ground, unnoticed. Gail remembered the urgency of her mission.

'Come on,' she said. 'Hurry!'

'Where are we going?' he wanted to know, 'It's getting late.'

She laughed provocatively, teasing him.

'There's a boat waiting. We're going to one of the islands — there's a hut where I'm hiding out.' She added, softly: 'We'll be alone there, Roy.'

He blushed.

'Gail! Don't you think — '

She kissed him into silence, asking:

'Don't you want me, Roy?'

His voice was hoarse. He trembled a little.

'I want to marry you, Gail.'

She laughed, caught his arm and dragged him after her, down the sloping bank to the water's edge. The moon shone again and she saw the waiting boat. Snowy was at the oars; she didn't see

Nugent. Neither did Belknap until too late.

The giant negro came softly from the shadow of the overhang on crepe-soled shoes. Belknap turned catching hot breath on his neck. He half-turned, caught a glimpse of gleaming white teeth and tiny bright eyes. He put up his arm to defend himself, crying out:

'Gail — look . . . '

Nugent's fist swung in a short arc. It hit Belknap full on the jaw, sent his head back with a crack: Belknap went over backwards onto the sand, forming a crumpled heap, unmoving, silent.

Gail snapped, wildly: 'You fool — you've killed him.'

Nugent grinned and bent over the still form of Roy Belknap. He felt for a pulse, said:

'No, Miss Gail. He sho is still with us. He ain't hurt — much, Ah guesses.'

Without effort, Nugent picked up the unconscious Belknap and tossed him into the boat. Gail stepped in, swearing as the water splashed her silk stockings.

Nugent pushed the boat into deeper

water and took the second pair of oars. The two men rowed in silence.

Gail fingered the diamond necklace round her throat, smiling at Roy's innocence. He'd walked into the trap without suspecting anything, had even bought her a gift — the sucker! She laughed; a low, harsh sound.

'He gave me these,' she said, pointing at the limp body in the bottom of the boat.

Snowy's wild eyes glinted, but he said nothing.

Nugent grinned.

'That sho is a fancy piece o' jewellery. He must be tickled pink on account of yo, Miss Gail.'

'Yeah!' Snowy's voice was savage. 'You dames only have to show off your figure to get anything out of a guy.' He seemed upset about it.

Gail laughed provocatively, letting the fur wrap slide off her bare shoulders. She stretched her long legs, showing silk hose in the moonlight. Both men looked at her, licked their lips — and said nothing.

Gail Gray laughed; she knew what they

were thinking and it amused her to tease them, knowing that neither of them dare try anything with Harvey Chandos's girlfriend. Snowy said something under his breath and pulled harder on the oars; it was his opinion that Chan's latest dame was a cold-blooded bitch without a spark of decent feeling in her body.

The boat was out in the current now and a cold wind blew up. Gail shivered, and hugged the fur about her slim figure. The moon came out again and, to the north, she could see the outline of ships in the dock basins. She thought Madame Popocopolis was smart in using Jamaica Bay as a hideout. Gail didn't like the fat woman, but she grudgingly admitted she had brains.

Jamaica Bay was a half-circle of water to the south of Queens, on Long Island, playground of New York City. The bay was shielded from the Atlantic breakers by Rockaway peninsula, jutting from the mainland, and bisected by Cross Bay Boulevard, running north-south from Howard Beach to Rockaway. The bay was dotted with sand bars, the home of duck and geese, happy hunting ground of sportsmen, and it was on one of these sandbanks that the hideout had been prepared. It was unlikely that anyone would discover their presence there. The boat was out in Broad Channel now and Rulers Bar Hassock, in the centre of the bay, was behind them. Silver Bar was somewhere ahead.

Roy Belknap came up from the bottom of the boat with fists clenched, hurling himself at Snowy, the nearest oarsman. Belknap had been conscious for several minutes, playing possum. He'd figured that the negro and the small man with the shock of hair were Gail's enemies, that they'd kidnapped her — and he intended to save her.

Snowy was taken completely by surprise. Belknap's fist smashed into his face and he went to the bottom of the boat, losing his oars. Gail cried out, startled:

'You fool, Roy — they'll kill you!'

Belknap misunderstood her. He still thought of her as a prisoner, thought she was worried for him. He went into the attack with renewed vigour. Nugent shipped his oars hurriedly and launched himself at Belknap. Gail sprang forward, dived for Belknap's legs, dragging him down, hampering him. Roy struggled with the giant, cursing, thinking Gail had mistaken him for one of the others in the excitement. He hammered his fists into Nugent's face.

Snowy came upright, spitting blood and swearing. He pushed Gail aside and grabbed an oar. He hit Belknap low down in the belly with the wooden shaft. Belknap moaned and vomited. His hands dropped to protect his stomach and Nugent caught him by the throat.

The negro was surprised and alarmed by the attack. His grip tightened, squeezing the air from Belknap's lungs. He was over seven feet tall, and broad to match — a giant with a giant's strength. He was panicky now, afraid someone would hear them. He crushed Belknap's neck in a steel vice, throttling him.

Gail cried: 'Don't kill him — for God's sake, don't kill him!'

Nugent hardly heard her. He bent Belknap backwards, straining, using all the force of his tremendous body, squeezing . . . Belknap felt his strength leave him. His body went limp; his arms dropped. His lungs were labouring for air, gasping with the torture of the void inside him. He couldn't breathe any more . . . a film of blackness spread over his eyes and rushing sound filled his ears. He never knew the precise moment when he died.

Nugent's face was a mask of savageness. Even after Belknap stopped struggling, he kept his massive hands clamped about his throat, squeezing tighter and tighter. He felt Gail hit him.

'Let go. Let go, you fool!' she screamed.

Nugent's hands relaxed. Belknap slithered to the boards and made a grotesque form that no living thing could have taken. Snowy said, hoarsely:

'Jeeze, he's a goner, all right. What you want to hold onto him like that for?'

Nugent licked his thick lips and looked down at the man he had killed. Fear suddenly began to fill his mind. Without thinking, he bent over and picked up the body, heaved it over the side. The corpse floated for a few seconds, then began to sink. The tide caught it, sucked it under. As the moon went behind a cloud the corpse of Roy Belknap disappeared from view.

Gail slumped on the seat in the darkness. A whimpering sound came from her lips, carmine in a white oval. Hardened as she was, it was the first time she'd seen a man killed, and she was frightened. Snowy snarled.

'Shut up, you bitch!'

Nugent sat down and took the oars. Automatically, he rowed in a circle, searching for the body, but it had sunk from view. He found Snowy's oars, drifting on the tide, and dragged them into the boat.

Snowy said: 'I guess we'd better head for Silver Bar and tell Chan.'

No one said anything for several minutes; they were all stunned by the catastrophe. The carefully laid plan had gone wrong; there would be no ransom for Roy Belknap now. Snowy and Nugent pulled on the oars while Gail sat stiff and silent, more scared than she'd been in her life. This was murder!

The boat beached on the sandy strip of Silver Bar and the moon came out long enough to show the duck-hunter's hut. There was no light, but all three knew that Chandos and the fat woman were waiting inside. Nugent shivered. He said:

'Ma'am ain't gonna like this, Ah guesses. No sir, Ah sho figures she ain't gonna like it one little bit!'

5

Johnny Fortune moved quickly. He switched on the light and darted across the large room with the tiger-decorated pile on the floor. The first door he opened led to a bedroom; empty, the bed had not been used. Frowning, he searched the other rooms of Harvey Chandos's penthouse apartment. He found no one. The place was deserted.

That was unexpected. Temporarily, Johnny was caught off-balance. He'd intended to snatch Gail Gray and race away with her before Chandos had time to think, relying on speed and the element of surprise to help him. But Gail and Chandos were out somewhere; probably a nightclub — it might be hours before they returned.

He went into the living room, lit a cigarette and helped himself to Chandos's whisky. He sat down to think. He could wait for Gail to return — but perhaps

Chandos might have company. Snowy carried a gun, and the giant Nugent looked as if he could take care of him with one hand. Johnny considered the idea of returning to Ava without her sister . . . and shook his head. Ava was relying on him and he couldn't disappoint her.

He made himself comfortable on the divan and switched off the light. His cigarette made faint red sparks in the darkness and the whisky gave him a warm glow inside. He grinned, imagining the shock Chandos would have when he returned. A clock struck one. Johnny Fortune caressed the handle of his swagger cane; if he twisted the handle, a keen steel blade would shoot out. More than one crook, thinking him unarmed because he never carried a gun, had been tricked by Johnny's swordstick. Perhaps he'd have need of it tonight . . .

His cigarette went out. He finished the whisky and relaxed, eyes wide, senses alert. The half-hour struck. He put his feet up and his head back, still gripping his cane. The minutes ticked by with agonizing slowness, and still the door did not open. Johnny yawned with boredom; he craved action, excitement — the waiting game did not suit him at all. But there was nothing else he could do.

He heard two o'clock strike. Chandos was making a night of it; well, that was okay. Chandos would not be expecting trouble and probably he'd have had a lot to drink. Johnny would have the edge on him. Moonlight filtered in through the curtained windows, making a silvery pattern in the shadows. Doubt began to form in Johnny's mind. He became restless. Where was Gail? Why didn't Chandos return? Johnny waited with growing uneasiness.

He heard three o'clock chime. The night was still and quiet. There was no traffic on the road outside. Johnny began to think of Ava, how she had slipped into his arms and returned his kiss. It was pleasant thinking of her, realizing that, for the first time, he was in love. When this business was over, he intended to ask her to marry him — and he thought he knew what her answer would be. Dreaming of the girl he loved, Johnny Fortune dozed, dropping into sleep. His eyes closed but he could still see Ava's loveliness, her bronze hair and soft brown eyes. He sighed contentedly in his sleep and his arms closed round a cushion . . .

He was cold and stiff and his hand was cramped round the handle of his cane. A red flush of light seeped in through the windows. Abruptly, Johnny Fortune was awake. He swung his feet off the divan and sat up. The clock told him it was some minutes after six in the morning. He cursed himself for being so careless as to fall asleep and went quickly through the apartment. No one had come in yet.

Johnny yawned and stretched. It had been a wasted night — but where was Gail Gray? He frowned wondering what had kept her and Chandos out all night. He pulled back the curtains to let in the dawn light. It was unlikely that Chandos would show up now; he might as well go back to his own apartment and tell Ava she'd have to wait till he learnt what had happened to her sister. Ava was going to worry about that.

He went through all the rooms carefully, looking for anything that might give him a clue to the missing occupants, and found nothing. Except a wall safe with a combination lock. Johnny grinned recklessly. There might be something worth discovering in the safe, and he didn't think he'd have much difficulty in opening it; he had once befriended a cracksman who had shown him a few tricks of the profession.

Johnny Fortune moved the dial, listening to the faint click of metallic tumblers. He turned slowly, listening intently. He felt the first tumbler fall into place, juggled the dial again. The second clicked home. He went on turning, listening with sensitive fingertips. The last tumbler clicked in place and he flung wide the safe door.

Inside, he found neatly stacked wads of dollar bills, a few bonds, and some jewellery — probably Gail's.

There were no papers of any kind; Harvey Chandos wasn't the sort of man to leave evidence of his criminal activities in such an obvious place.

Johnny filled his pockets with green-backs and selected a bracelet and ruby-studded necklace for Ava. Grinning, he scribbled a message for Chandos, placing it inside the safe:

Expenses for a wasted night — J.F.

When Chandos found that, he wouldn't go to the police. A crook is always wary of calling in the cops — when his money has not been made honestly. Johnny let himself out of the penthouse and took the elevator to the ground floor. The night clerk had his feet up and a newspaper over his eyes; Johnny didn't disturb him. He got into his coupé and drove back to Long Island City.

Ava Gray let him in again. She looked relieved to see him, slipped into his arms and let him kiss her. She murmured:

'Oh, Johnny — I thought something had happened to you.'

She realized he was alone. Her voice faltered:

'Gail?'

Johnny released her, shrugged.

'Your guess is as good as mine. The

birds have flown. No one showed up all night.'

Ava was worried. 'Do you think something has happened to her?'

'Stop worrying. They probably had a merry evening and decided to make a night of it. They'll be back — then I'll go get your sister. We can't do anything till then, so calm down.'

She managed to control her fears, smiled at him,

'I've just spent a night in a man's apartment — and I don't feel bad about it.'

Johnny laughed: 'I wish I'd been here!'

She blushed, moved away to the kitchen.

'I'll get breakfast, Johnny. You rest, then we can talk about Gail. How will we find her, now?'

'Leave that to me. You concentrate on bacon and eggs — I want to find out what sort of a wife you'll make.'

Johnny Fortuue relaxed in a chair, wondering what the devil had happened to keep Chandos and Gail away all night. He hoped it was nothing bad; but a little nagging doubt crept into his mind. Perhaps he was already too late to help Gail.

Perhaps Ava would never see her sister again.

* * *

'You fools!' snarled Madame Popocopolis. 'You stupid, incompetent fools!' Her piggy eyes blazed with fury and the rolls of fat comprising her grotesque body shook with anger. 'To have twenty million dollars almost in my hands, then to have it thrown away by fools! To kill him was bad enough — but to throw the body into the water, for anyone to find . . . that was madness! Nugent, I ought to whip every inch of skin off your stupid body!'

The giant shrank back, fear showing in the whites of his eyes. He trembled before the fat woman. Never had he seen her so angry before.

'Ah'm sho sorry, ma'am,' he whined. 'Ah didn't mean to kill him. It was just that Ah forgets mah own strength. Ah just sort o' put mah hands round his neck and he dies. He ain't no right to die so easy — it isn't fair.'

Snowy's thin face twitched nervously.

71

Hands trembling, he opened a paper packet and took a pinch of white powder between his fingers; he held the powder to his nostrils and inhaled. The dope helped, calmed his nerves. He moved forward from the shadows behind Nugent and stood in the pool of light cast by an oil-lamp.

'Belknap took us by surprise,' he said. 'We thought he was out cold. When he jumped us, we didn't have time to think. It was bad luck Nugent croaking him — it couldn't be helped.'

Madame Popocopolis's ugly face formed a sneer.

'It was just bad luck you lost the body — it couldn't be helped that you threw away twenty million bucks!'

Harvey Chandos's red face had turned a dirty grey. His bloated jowls shook like alarm signals.

'We have to get away, back to the apartment, get an alibi. This is murder! I told you we shouldn't have pulled this snatch — now look at the mess we're in. We've got to — '

'Shut up!' Madame Popocopolis glared

at the bookmaker with contempt. 'We'll stay here for two or three days — no one knows we're here. It'll give us the chance to see how things work out. I've no intention of going to the chair for the blunder of a pair of fools!'

Chandos regained some of his nerve. He chewed the end off a cigar and lit up. He knew the fat woman had the brains of the outfit; if she had a plan, he felt better.

Gail Gray calmed down too. She had got over her fear; now she knew a cold excitement. The gang had committed murder — and she was in it up to the neck. It was a pity Roy was dead; she'd intended to make Chandos doublecross Madame Popocopolis once they had the money. That would have to wait. She, too, knew that only the fat woman's brains could save them.

She fitted a cigarette in her black jade holder and blew a stream of smoke across the cellar under the hut on Silver Bar. Her bronze hair was limp from water spray, her silk stockings ruined; nevertheless, she had control of herself now, and she knew she had to fight Madame Popocopolis's power over Harvey.

She drawled: 'I think Harvey's right.' She smiled at him with curving, carmined lips and swayed her lovely body enticingly. 'What's wrong with going back to the apartment? No one knows we had anything to do with Roy Belknap.'

The fat woman cackled hideously, leering at her

'You'd like to get Harvey away from me, would you, dearie? Well, you won't! Harvey knows which side his bread's buttered. I'm the only one who can save his crooked neck!'

Gail looked beseechingly at Chandos. The bookmaker said:

'Gail's right — the cops have got nothing on us. We're in the clear.'

'Are we?' The fat woman laughed again. 'As soon as Belknap's body is found, the cops are going to hunt up everyone who knew him. It won't take them long to find out he was in love with Gail. Remember the diamond necklace he gave her? He bought that recently — the cops are going to start looking for the girl.

And she'll lead them to us.'

Gail stared at the giant Nugent with cold eyes.

'We can give them Nugent,' she said. 'He did the killing.'

Madame Popocopolis's double chins quivered.

'You fool! I'd sacrifice Nugent to the cops — or you, or Harvey — if it would do any good. But it won't. We'd all be gaoled as accomplices to a murder rap. Old man Belknap doted on his only son; *he* won't be satisfied till we're all inside — and his millions give him plenty of pull with the D.A.'

Chandos frowned: 'Yeah, we're all in this together.'

The fat woman smiled at him.

'There's something else. Roy Belknap's body may not be discovered immediately — that gives us a chance to collect. The cops aren't going to know we haven't got the boy a prisoner until he's fished out of the water. That's why we're gonna sit tight for a couple of days.'

Snowy's face lit up.

'Yeah, maybe we can still get that

twenty million bucks!'

Nugent grunted: 'Ah guesses it don't matter so much after all that Ah croaked that fellar . . . '

The fat woman looked round the cellar, satisfied now she was in control again — but she wasn't going to like much more of Gail's impudence. The girl would have to go — she was a menace to their security.

She said: 'If the body doesn't turn up, we'll put pressure on old man Belknap — make him pay up, then hop over the border. But we stay here till we know.' Chandos nodded.

'That sounds okay.'

Gail dragged on her cigarette. She said:

'*If* Belknap isn't found — what happens if he is?'

★   ★   ★

Dawn found Ed Lowery on Little Egg Marsh, in Jamaica Bay, cursing the ducks who kept out of range of his gun. Water had spilled into the top of his waders, soaking his feet. An icy wind chilled his hands, penetrating his wind-breaker as he lay on his stomach in the reeds near the water's edge, gun poking up at the red sky.

Ed had been there all night, cursing the contrary birds who kept away from his hide-hole. He hadn't lined his sights on one duck during the six hours he'd been there; hadn't pulled trigger once. It looked as if he was right out of luck. He rubbed his whiskers with a gnarled hand, bones creaking in his old body. A man needed to be young for this caper, he thought disgustedly.

A ship's siren whistled in the distance; the first sound of day. Ed got to his feet, waders squelching unpleasantly; he knew the ducks wouldn't settle now. Soon, the bay would be alive with ships and men and noise. He'd have to wait for another night to bag a brace of ducks. He unloaded his gun, shoved the cartridges in his pocket and slung a haversack over his shoulder.

His boat was a hundred yards upstream, hidden under a foliage of reeds. He started up, pushing his way through the tall weeds, when his legs bumped into something in the water. He looked down and saw a face.

Ed Lowery said: 'Jesus wept,' and nearly jumped out of his waders. He bent over and disturbed the weeds, grabbing a cold wet hand; he knew then why the ducks hadn't settled that night — they didn't like a corpse any more than Ed Lowery did. He pulled the body onto the sand and looked it over.

It had been a young man, with blond hair and a handsome face. Its clothes had cost a lot of money, which made Ed feel through the pockets. A wallet contained a thousand bucks — and the wristwatch was shockproof and waterproof. Ed felt he was entitled to the watch and the money, so he took them. After all, it had been a bad night for duck.

There were deep black thumb-marks on the neck; that added up to murder to Ed. A police job. The body hadn't been in the water long; probably the man — a printed card gave his name as Roy Belknap and an address in Suffolk — had been killed that same night, while Ed had been lying in wait for ducks.

Ed dragged the body to his boat, dumped it in the bottom, and took the oars. He'd heard the cops paid a reward to the finder of bodies, and he intended to cash in on this one. No one need know he'd taken the money and watch; the murderer would be the obvious suspect.

He rowed steadily for fifteen minutes while the wind dropped and the sun came up. It was going to be another hot summer day. He crossed Beach Channel to Rockaway, hauled the boat up onto the sand and started looking for a cop. A call box brought him a patrolman mounted on a motorcycle; a young cop keen for promotion. The young cop liked the idea of handling a murder.

He, too, saw the thumb-marks and jumped to conclusions; the empty wallet confirmed his opinion.

'Murder with violence,' he stated authoritatively. 'Motive — money.'

His face flushed when he saw the name and address.

'Holy cow — Thad Belknap's one and only!'

'You know him?' Ed Lowery asked, lighting his pipe and puffing on it, unimpressed by the young cop.

'I'll say! Don't you read the papers? This is Roy Belknap, only son of Thaddeus Belknap, multi-millionaire and then some. This is a big break for me. Stay with the body, Lowery — I've got some phoning to do.'

He was back in ten minutes, flushed and excited. He got out a notebook and started questioning Ed Lowery. Fifteen minutes went by before Homicide arrived with the meat-wagon. After that, the young cop took a back seat. There was a bustle of activity; flashlights and photographs; measurements and finger-prints; questions and more questions. The cops looked out across Jamaica Bay, at the marshes and sand bars, and shook their heads solemnly. It was going to be a tough one to crack. But it would have to be cracked; Thad Belknap would see to that. The D.A. would be running round in circles before the day was out.

A lieutenant said:

'Roy Belknap murdered — now things will move!'

'Yeah,' said another. 'This means the dragnet — Homicide dragnet!'

6

The doorbell buzzed insistently. Johnny Fortune left a comfortable chair and crossed his apartment, wondering who was calling. It could hardly be Ava, she had only left for her hotel an hour previously. Johnny had lunched alone and was enjoying a cigarette and a rye when the bell buzzed.

He opened the door to see the stooped, thin body of Lieutenant Dix, of Homicide. Dix's high-pitched silky voice said quietly:

'Business, Johnny.'

The lieutenant wandered in, looking round the apartment with casually careless eyes, but missing nothing. Johnny poured Dix a drink, noticed, as he had many times before, the red stump of a missing finger on Dix's left hand.

They sat down, facing each other. Johnny didn't like the expression on the lieutenant's face. There was a lack of friendliness about the eyes behind horn-rimmed glasses. Dix pushed his hat up and back and drank the whisky in one draught, placing the empty glass carefully on the small table between them.

His face, with circular glasses and a hat with an upturned brim, was owlish; but the brain behind the face was keen and sure. Johnny knew that Dix didn't miss any bets; he was a good cop.

'Well, Dix,' Johnny said, drawing on his cigarette, 'what can I do for you? And don't look at me as if I'd committed a murder. We're old friends aren't we?'

Dix's smile was too cold, too automatic. Johnny moved uneasily, instantly wary. The lieutenant said:

'Roy Belknap's body was fished out of Jamaica Bay this morning. He'd been strangled.'

Johnny said: 'So? I'd heard of him, of course — who hasn't? But I'd never met him. Tough for his old man. You don't think I had anything to do with it?'

Dix said: 'You know where I can find Chandos and Gail Gray?'

The question hit Johnny Fortune

without warning. His light blue eyes went deliberately blank; his debonair manner deserted him for the moment. He brushed tobacco grains from his trim moustache thinking fast — Ava had to be kept out of this.

'I can't tell you, Dix. I don't know. I take it you've checked the Myrtle Avenue address?'

The lieutenant nodded.

'The place is empty and they won't be back. We've done a lot of checking, Johnny, and the leads point to Chandos and his girlfriend. Yesterday, you were interested in them — particularly the girl. Why? You haven't got some fool notion of trying to protect her, have you?'

Johnny shrugged carelessly.

'I'd no idea Gail knew Roy Belknap — this is all news to me. If I could help you, I would, but I know nothing about it. Nothing at all, Dix.'

'You wouldn't hold out on me, Johnny?'

'Suppose you tell me what you've learned so far? What makes you think Chandos is involved?'

Johnny Fortune leaned back in his chair, relaxed, ready to match wits with the lieutenant. He wanted to know how deeply Gail Gray was involved; whether he'd be able to help Ava's sister. Dix spoke in his high-pitched, silky voice.

'Belknap was found at dawn by a man named Lowery. He'd been duck-hunting on Little Egg Marsh and found the body tangled in the weeds. He rowed the body across to Rockaway and called the cops — ' Dix scowled. 'A youngster went out, thought he was all set for promotion. The body had been robbed, so he jumped to conclusions. The Homicide boys thought the patrolman had grilled Lowery — and he hadn't. We lost three hours before someone got the notion it was Lowery who'd helped himself to Belknap's wallet — after the killing.'

Dix sighed.

'That gave us a new approach. Obviously, Belknap hadn't been murdered by a chance hold-up man, as we'd thought — and the delay gave the murderers time to beat it. What was Belknap doing out there last night?

Cherchez la femme! The way we figure it now, is that the girl lured him out there and the gang would hold him to ransom. A kidnap job. Belknap must have put up a fight and was accidentally killed. I bet they're mad about that — no ransom money to come — and a murder rap to face when they're caught. That it was probably accidental means nothing; old Thaddeus Belknap will see that they burn for it. He's down at City Hall now, raising hell with the D.A. This city will be turned upside down in the next few days. The gang haven't a chance of getting away.'

'And Chandos?' Johnny prompted.

Dix said: 'Like I told you, when we got this new angle, we started making enquiries. Roy Belknap had been staying at Greystones Hotel on Astoria Boulevard. He'd been acting like a sick puppy on account of Gail Grey turned him down a while back. We can find no other girl in his life since then — so that makes her a key suspect. Last night, he gets a 'phone call — we haven't got a line on that yet, but it seems certain it was from the girl.

'He rushed out and bought a diamond necklace for twenty thousand bucks. He left the hotel about ten o'clock last night — that was the last time he was seen alive. Gail Gray has been going with Chandos since she turned Belknap down — and their apartment is empty. That adds up to me.'

Johnny tried not to look worried. Ava wasn't going to like this. Dix rose to his feet, fixed Johnny with a cold stare, and said:

'Come clean, Johnny — don't hold out on me.'

Johnny Fortune stubbed out his cigarette. He said:

'I had private business with Chandos — nothing to do with this killing. I knew nothing at all about Roy Belknap — and that's the truth, Dix. Chandos was at his apartment yesterday evening. I haven't seen him since then and I don't know where he is.'

The lieutenant sauntered to the door, pulled down his hat.

'Okay, Johnny, if that's how you want it.'

He sighed again, and went out, closing the door after him.

Johnny Fortune poured himself another rye and tossed it back. He grimaced, feeling sorry for Ava. He didn't think there was much he could do for Gail now, but he was still prepared to try, because he was in love with Ava. Somehow he had to protect her from the shock this was going to be; he knew that if the cops got a line on her, she'd be in for a grilling. The D.A wasn't going to believe it was just coincidence that she was in New York at the time her sister was involved in kidnapping and murder.

Johnny picked up his cane and left the apartment. He couldn't go to Ava's hotel without putting the cops on her trail; he'd 'phone from a public booth. The elevator took him swiftly downwards and he collected his coupé, driving along Vernon to the intersection with Astoria Boulevard. He used a call box in a drug store and dialled Ava's hotel number. When she answered, he said crisply:

'Listen carefully, Ava. Gail's in a jam with the police. There's been a murder, and she may be involved. I'll do what I can to help her, but I want you to stay under cover. Don't try to get in touch with me — I'll ring you when I have news. The man who got killed was Roy Belknap and his father's a millionaire several times over; that means things are going to hum until the killers are brought in. If the cops find you're Gail's sister, you'll be in for a bad time. So sit tight and try not to worry too much. Remember, I'm working for you.'

He rang off quickly, not wanting to answer questions until he knew more. He went out and sat in his car, thinking. It was hot; bright sunlight bathed the wide concrete boulevard and girls in thin summer dresses passed by on their way to the beach. Johnny thought of the Greystones Hotel, remembering he knew the telephone operator; Vi, the blonde he'd met at Belmont Park the day before. That was a stroke of luck; she'd tell him anything she knew.

He started the coupé's engine and drove east along Astoria. Greystones looked as its name implied; a tall granite building, grey and weathered, with a discreet foyer and total absence of chromium and glitter. It was an expensive place, catering for big names who wanted anonymity. When Johnny arrived there were cops all over the place and the manager looked harassed. The D.A. had turned loose a lot of men for this job; Thad Belknap insisted on results and he had the money to back his play.

Johnny slipped into the telephone operator's room and closed the door behind him. He said, smiling:

'Hello, Vi — back any winners yesterday?'

Vi Maitland spun round in her chair. She was tall and young and good looking, a blonde who knew how to dress well, but right now there was a little furrow about her eyes. It might have been worry or fear — but the moment she recognized the slim, debonair figure of Johnny Fortune, her eyes lit up with relief. She said, breathlessly:

'Johnny, am I glad to see you!'

He smiled encouragingly, swinging his cane.

'Are you, gorgeous? Tell Johnny what's worrying you. Something to do with the Belknap killing?'

She nodded eagerly.

'I can't tell the police, Johnny, and I know I ought. You know how strict the management is about — well, overhearing telephone conversations — and I can't afford to lose this job. You see, I was on duty last night, and — '

Johnny leaned forward, tensed but still smiling.

'And you heard what passed between Roy Belknap and Gail Gray. All right, Vi — let's have it!'

Her face crimsoned.

'It's the first time, Johnny, believe me. I don't make a habit of listening in on 'phone calls, but he was Roy Belknap and — well, I guess I had a bit of a crush on him. I was curious about this girl. Anyway, I heard her make the rendezvous and I know the police would want me to tell them — only I can't . . . because I'd lose my job. But you can tell them without saying I told you, can't you?'

Johnny grinned.

'Don't worry, gorgeous — just give me the news. I'll take it from there.'

Vi sighed with relief, gulped, and began:

'It was Gail Gray who 'phoned Roy. She said she wanted him to meet her because she was in trouble; she was cooing like a dove, telling him she loved him — and he lapped it up, the dope! He was to meet her at Goose Creek station in Jamaica Bay at eleven o'clock; he was to take a single rail ticket and tell no one where he was going. I guess he fell for it, all right — and now he's dead. Poor Roy!'

Johnny whistled under his breath. It looked as if Dix was right; the set-up smelled of a kidnap job with Gail as bait. Well, she deserved all she'd get when the cops caught up with her. Then he remembered Ava and his expression softened — maybe he could beat the cops and get Gail across the border, leaving Chandos to take the rap.

He'd be breaking the law, but he was prepared to do that for Ava. He kissed Vi lightly and turned away.

'Stop worrying, gorgeous; Johnny will

take care of everything — and don't mention this little chat to the cops. Bye, now.'

He went out to his coupé and got behind the wheel.

The car moved away from the curb, into the flux of traffic on Astoria Boulevard, travelling east. Johnny kept his foot hard down; with a police dragnet in operation, he had no time to lose if he was to save Gail.

He swung right at the Connecting Highway and headed south, turning left at the Queens Broadway. Traffic signals held him up at the junction of Roosevelt and Broadway and he had time to consider how peaceful it was compared with Manhattan's brightly-lit strip of theatre-land.

The lights changed to green and the coupé shot forward, winding in and out of the traffic. He turned south again at Woodhaven Boulevard and stepped on the accelerator; he had a wide road and a clear run now. Heat waves shimmered in the air and the bright sunlight made the concrete glitter. He passed St. John's

Cemetery, flashed over the Union Turnpike and went through Forest Park.

At the bottom of Woodhaven, he picked up Cross Bay Boulevard. Shellbank Basin was on his left, ships being unloaded in the docks; then he was out over the glittering sunlit water, a mirror of blue, unbroken and dead-calm. As he crossed the steel bridge, he glimpsed police launches patrolling the bay, searching the marshes and sand banks.

The bridge brought him to Rulers Bar Hassock and he turned down the dry mud track leading to Goose Creek station. Johnny didn't bother the railroad man but left the coupé and started searching the shore for tracks. There would be no point in bringing Belknap here unless they intended taking him over the water.

Police helicopters were in the air over the bay, but so far, the cops hadn't got around to Goose Creek; the body had been found in the south part of the bay and they were covering that area first. Johnny walked along the rocky shore, stopping every now and again to look at the sand. He found no footprints; but then they'd keep to the rock and the water would have washed all marks from the sand.

A leather case caught his eye. He picked it up, excitement building up in him. It had been a jewel case and the makers were Pearce & Mason of Astoria Boulevard; Johnny felt sure he was on the right track. Dix had said that Belknap had bought Gail a diamond necklace and this was the right sort of case.

Johnny stared across the bay. In the distance, beyond Broad Channel was Silver Bar; that was the most likely place they'd head for from this point. All he wanted now was a boat . . .

He turned, hearing footsteps on the rock behind him. Lieutenant Dix, the D.A., and another man Johnny didn't know were coming towards him. Behind them were half-a-dozen uniformed cops, one with a walkie-talkie radio.

Dix said: 'Hi, Johnny, you sure get around. What you found there?'

The D.A., Tim Wilson, was stout and dark with close-cropped hair and a sharp, pointed nose, dressed in blue serge that was well-worn. He said:

'What's your interest in this business, Fortune? Mr. Belknap, this is Johnny Fortune.'

Johnny looked at the millionaire. Thaddeus Belknap had a grey face and a cold glitter in his eyes; he looked like a man wanting revenge and wanting it badly. He was tall and powerful, nearly bald, immaculately dressed in expensive clothes and smelling faintly of perfume. Johnny nodded to him and handed the leather case to Dix. He said:

'I just found this. I figure this is where they had the boat waiting — and Silver Bar looks like a good hideout. How did you get here anyway?'

Dix inspected the case, nodded grimly.

'You've found it, Johnny. We're doing a routine check of the area. Someone used this station last night — a single ticket from Astoria was left at the ticket office — no one on duty at that time of night. It all adds up to Roy Belknap. How did you get onto this, if it's not a secret?'

Johnny grinned.

'I'm afraid it is.'

The D.A. said, sharply: 'This is murder, Fortune. Hold out on the department and I'll pull you in!'

'My source of information has nothing to do with the crime, Wilson; I'm sure of that. All I heard was the mention of Goose Creek, and I came out to investigate. You've got the result in your hand — I'm holding back nothing.'

Thad Belknap stepped forward, glittering eyes fixed on Johnny's face. His voice was harsh, embittered.

'I'm going to get the murderers of my son if it takes the rest of my life and all my money. That boy meant everything to me — all I have left is vengeance . . . and, by God, I'm going to have it! His murderers will go to the electric chair!'

Belknap's grey face took on the appearance of a cadaver, grim and threatening.

'I'll pay good money for anything leading to the killers' capture, starting now. Fortune, here's ten grand — ' He pulled out his wallet, thrust the notes at Johnny. 'I'll pay for everything you can tell me.'

97

Johnny ignored the money. His voice was cold with pride.

'I don't have to be bribed to help the police. I don't like murder any more than you do — and I'm sorry for you, Mr. Belknap. I'll do anything I can to help catch Chandos and the gang — but I don't want your money.'

Dix pushed his hat up and back. He said:

'Let's get out to Silver Bar. We're wasting time.' He ordered the cop with the walkie-talkie: 'Get a launch here, son.'

The cop spoke into his radio and, far out across the bay, a high-speed police launch turned and headed for Goose Creek. Its bow made a spray of white foam as it cleaved the water. The launch pulled into the creek and Johnny leapt aboard her. Lieutenant Dix, the D.A. and Thad Belknap followed, and the launch moved out to deeper water. Dix said to the man at the wheel:

'Silver Bar.'

The launch picked up speed, sending a fine spray of water over the bow, onto the men in the cockpit. Johnny stared ahead, at the flat expanse of sandy rock that was Silver Bar. He wondered if Gail was there, and his lips tightened. He couldn't save Ava's sister now . . .

The launch beached and the cops circled the wooden shack, guns covering the door and windows. Dix called:

'All right, the game's up Chandos. Come out with your hands in the air.'

There was no answer. The cops moved in and Dix flung wide the door. Johnny followed him in. The hut was empty, walls and floor bare as if it hadn't been used for weeks.

'Too late,' the D.A. said. 'The birds have flown. Well, they won't get far. The area is cordoned and the dragnet will get 'em.'

Dix's eyes gleamed behind horn-rimmed spectacles and he lost his owlish expression. He snapped:

'Wait — there's a trapdoor here. We'll take a look at the cellar.'

Johnny Fortune held his breath. It seemed that Gail Gray was past helping now. Lieutenant Dix pulled up the trapdoor and stared into the cellar.

7

Gail Gray found little comfort in Chandos's arms in the cellar on Silver Bar. The room was small, sparsely furnished; the air was hot and stuffy, the yellow light of the oil lamp a strain to the eyes. She was used to comfort and she didn't have it here.

Several hours had passed since she'd arrived with the news of Roy Belknap's death. Chandos was on edge; Snowy used dope to calm his nerves while they waited; Nugent kept in the background, trying to avoid the penetrating eyes of Madame Popocopolis — he knew he couldn't escape the hot seat if they were found. Only the fat woman seemed able to relax, to ignore the tension that had built up.

Gail jabbed a cigarette in the end of her long jade holder and flicked the wheel of a lighter. She inhaled deeply, forcing herself to keep quiet; she knew that if she opened her mouth she'd scream. She wanted to get away from Silver Bar, far away — but she wasn't going to let Madame Popocopolis get Harvey alone and poison his mind against her. She knew how much the fat woman hated her.

Chandos fiddled with a radio set, trying first the commercial stations, then the police wavelength. They were waiting to hear if Belknap's body had been found . . .

The announcer on N.B.C. was excited. His voice jumped, garbled a torrent of words at high speed:

'Special news flash: Roy Belknap, only son of Thaddeus Belknap of Suffolk, Long Island — murdered! Belknap junior's body was pulled from the waters of Jamaica Bay exactly one hour ago. He had been strangled. The District Attorney, Mr. Wilson, states that the dragnet is out for the murderer; an arrest is expected within hours. Thaddeus Belknap, the well-known millionaire who made his money from — '

Chandos switched off the radio with trembling hands.

'We've got to get away from here. I knew it was a mistake to stay — '

'Shut up!' Madame Popocopolis's voice shrilled sharply and she heaved her gargantuan bulk in the chair. Her piggy eyes moved over the faces of her accomplices. She spoke again:

'We'll leave — now. There is no longer any chance of collecting ransom and the police will soon discover this hideout, now that Belknap's death is tied to this area. Fortunately, we have another hideout prepared. Harvey, get ready to leave immediately.'

Chandos pulled himself together.

'You mean, the 59th Avenue address?'

The fat woman snorted with impatience: 'Of course!'

Nugent and Snowy went up the steps to make ready the boat. Madame Popocopolis heaved her bulk onto the steps, panting with her exertions; she wasn't built for climbing. Gail fretted below, impatient to get out of the cellar; she felt cooped up, wanted to see the sky again, to breath fresh air. Chandos followed her up the steps as the fat woman reached the floor of the hut.

Outside, the sky was clearing and the breeze had dropped. The water was calm, grey-blue in the early morning light; it was going to be another hot day. Gail and Chandos huddled in the bow; Nugent and Snowy took the oars; Madame Popocopolis sat in the stern — the boat dipped heavily at that end as they pushed off.

'North-east,' the fat woman directed. 'Head for the pier at 165th.'

The giant's back arched and beads of sweat stood out on his dark face; Snowy pulled hard on the oars. Both knew they had no time to lose to get clear of the bay before police launches combed the area. The oars dipped and splashed as the boat headed for the mainland.

Chandos watched the sky anxiously; as yet, there was no sign of police helicopters, but he knew they wouldn't be long in taking up the chase.

'Faster,' he urged. 'Row faster!'

Gail's face was bright with excitement. She knew the danger they ran, but the thrill of being hunted overcame her fear. She held herself stiffly and golden flecks swirled in her brown eyes. Madame Popocopolis watched the girl. She thought: Is it time to get rid of Gail? It would be so easy to have her thrown over the side . . . No, she decided; the cops' only lead to them was through the girl. Later, perhaps, would be the time to throw her to the hunters — not now.

Ahead of the boat, the pier loomed; a drab concrete block jutting from the mainland. There was no one about as they tied up and mounted the steps to 165th Avenue. Chandos had left the Airflow at a garage on the corner; he made straight for it, trembling with eagerness.

Madame Popocopolis shook his arm.

'Not the Airflow,' she said. 'It will be recognised — take another car.' She stared round the garage, at the cars. 'That black saloon,' she directed, pointing.

Chandos got in, started the engine as a mechanic, greasy-faced and clad in overalls with a spanner in his hand, came up.

'You've got the wrong car, mister,' he called.

The fat woman cackled with laughter. She said:

'Take him, Nugent!'

The giant grinned, and grabbed the mechanic. He caught his collar with one hand, slammed his other fist into the mechanic's face. The man grunted, spat out blood. He didn't know what this was all about, but he wasn't going to be beaten up without a fight. He swung the spanner and aimed at Nugent's head.

Nugent ducked, grabbed the mechanic's arm and twisted — the man howled with pain and dropped the spanner. Nugent brought up his knee, viciously, drove it into the mechanic's groin. The man doubled up, eyes watering, clutching his belly.

Gail danced with excitement, lusting for blood. She wanted Nugent to kill . . .

'Kill him, Nugent,' she croaked hoarsely. 'Kill him for me!'

Nugent swung the mechanic off the ground, straightened up. The muscles of his arms rippled; he crashed the limp body against the concrete floor. The mechanic's skull cracked and blood ran out; he lay motionless. Nugent grinned broadly and flexed his arms.

'Easy,' he boasted. 'He broke too easy for mah — Ah likes a tough guy to fight.'

'Get in the car,' Madame Popocopolis snapped.

They piled in. Chandos took the wheel with Snowy and Nugent beside him. Gail was crushed in the back with Madame Popocopolis. The two women ignored each other.

Chandos drove the black saloon up Farmer's Boulevard, travelling fast. There were few people about; workmen going to the docks; a water-cart spraying the dusty streets; a boy delivering papers. The fat woman said:

'Drive slower, Harvey. We don't want to be conspicuous — and we can't afford to have a speed cop on our track.'

Chandos eased his foot off the accelerator, cursing under his breath. Instinctively, he wanted to get away from the bay as fast as he could; he didn't know how soon the police would cordon the area, how long it would be before he ran into a road block — but he realized that Madame Popocopolis was right. They couldn't afford to look as if they were in a hurry.

He drove north, into the Queens section of New York, crossing Sunrise Highway and passing Jamaica Race Track. He swung the black saloon left at Merrick Boulevard, skirting St. Albans' Golf club; two enthusiasts were driving off the green as the car sped by. Neither looked up.

Chandos had the car radio on, tuned to the police wavelength. Orders hummed over the ether, ordering patrol cars to ring the bay area. Things were moving; Thad Belknap was putting pressure on the D.A. to find the killers of his son. Automatically, Chandos urged the saloon to greater speed. No one spoke as the car roared across the junction at Hillside Avenue and swung left along Home Lawn Street to pick up Fresh Meadow Lane.

They were out of the danger area now. Chandos slowed down, lit a cigar. His face began to smile again. He swung left on the North Hempstead Turnpike, driving between St. Mary's Cemetery and the Kissena Park golf course. He turned down 170th Street to reach 59th Avenue, watching for the hideout.

The house had a 'To Let' sign outside, but that meant nothing; Madame Popocopolis had bought the house months ago in readiness for this moment. A red stone bungalow, it backed onto the cemetery; four blocks of dingy dwelling houses cut a U-shape into the graveyard, isolating the section from the main highway. Giant elms overhung the walls, almost hiding the house from view; it was a splendid hideout, with a back exit between the gravestones.

There were no eyes to see Chandos drive the saloon into the wooden garage at the rear of the bungalow. He locked the doors and they went into the house. The back rooms on the ground floor, and a cellar, were furnished, the windows screened so that no one would suspect the place was occupied.

Harvey Chandos chewed on the end of his cigar, smiling and confident. He said:

'We're safe enough here. No one knows

about this hideout.'

Nugent was silent; he knew they were thinking this was his fault; it gave him an uneasy feeling. Snowy took another dose of heroin to steady his nerves; the wild light went out of his eyes and he relaxed. Maybe they were safe here — he hoped so. One thing was certain; they couldn't move out into the open until the dragnet had passed them by.

Madame Popocopolis eased her bulk into a padded chair; it groaned under her weight. She smirked at Gail.

'A nice little love nest, eh dearie . . . '

Gail Gray watched Harvey. Maybe now was the time to get rid of the fat woman. Perhaps he would set Nugent to strangle Madame Popocopolis if she demanded it as a price for her favours.

'Yes,' she said slowly. 'The perfect love nest!'

8

Night dropped a blanket of darkness over Manhattan. In a hotel room on East 43rd Street, Ava Gray waited by the telephone. Restlessly she paced the room, drew the curtain and looked out over Grand Central to the lofty skyscraper of Radio City. Below, on Third Avenue, New York's millions swarmed, milling on sidewalks, dining in brightly-lit snack bars, released from work and out for an evening's enjoyment.

Some would make for Central Park, lovers arm-in-arm; others were heading for Broadway and the glamour of the theatre; others crossed the East River; for the noise and gaiety of Coney Island. But Ava Gray stayed in her room, waiting for the call that never came.

Johnny Fortune had telephoned once more since he'd told her the bad news of her sister and the killing of Roy Belknap. The police had found the hideout in the cellar in Jamaica Bay, but the birds had flown. Ava breathed with relief, knowing her sister was still free. Johnny had told her they'd found the boat and Chandos's Airflow, and the body of a dead mechanic. Even now the police were searching for a stolen black saloon, the getaway car. The Queens area of the city was isolated; no one could leave without a police check — it seemed only a matter of time before Chandos and Gail were caught. And Johnny, still with the police, did not 'phone her . . .

The radio news-commentators filled the air with bulletins about the progress of the police search. Descriptions of Gail and Chandos had been sent over the air, along with those of Madame Popocopolis, Snowy and Nugent. Thad Belknap had bought airtime to broadcast an appeal; he offered one hundred thousand dollars for information leading to the capture of the gang.

Ava paced the room, thinking of Gail and wondering why Johnny didn't call her. She thought back over what she knew of her sister's life in New York, trying to think where she could be. Ava wanted to go to her and offer to help her . . . but how could she find Gail when the police and Johnny Fortune had failed?

A name jogged her memory. The Smiler. She remembered that Chandos's name had been linked with a man called The Smiler. If she could find him, perhaps he could tell her where to go. She went through Gail's letters, searching for his address; it was contained in one of her early letters, written soon after she had met Chandos. The Smiler was a photographer for whom Gail had worked; it was through him that she had met Harvey Chandos. Ava found the address: 7b India Street, Greenpoint.

Hurriedly, Ava studied a map of New York. Greenpoint was in Queens, on Long Island, across the East River from Manhattan. She put on her coat, pushed some money into a handbag and scribbled a message for Johnny; she was going to find Gail somehow. She saw the bracelet and ruby-studded necklace Johnny had removed from Chandos's safe; on impulse, she put them on before leaving the hotel.

On the sidewalk, Ava mingled with the crowd, avoiding the brightly lit places. She found a cab outside Grand Central and gave the India Street address. The cab moved off, cut down Park Avenue and 36th, to St. Gabriels Park and the Queens Midtown Tunnel.

Traffic rumbled through the concrete arch of the tunnel, travelling under the river. It was a strange subterranean world; one continuous flow of cars jammed bumper to bumper in the harsh glare of electric lighting; engines throbbed, reverberating in the close confines of the tunnel, the air filled with gasoline fumes. Ava was glad when they came out on Long Island, on Borden Avenue.

The police were checking all cars leaving Queens, watching for the gang; no one bothered with the cars going into the search area and Ava's cab was not stopped. The cab turned right and south to Manhattan Avenue, crossing Newtown Creek by the overhead bridge. India Street was off to the right in Greenpoint, a narrow, drab street leading to the docks.

It was near enough the river for Ava to hear the water lapping at the pier. She asked the driver to wait and turned to the tumbledown house, searching for the right entrance.

It was down a flight of area steps. There was a pile of litter and a smell of rotten fruit; a faded sign said:

Photographic Studio.

Ava rang the bell and waited in the darkness.

Presently footsteps sounded and the door moved silently open to emit a faint yellow light. The man who looked at Ava had lecherous eyes and thin lips parted in a permanent, toothy smile. The Smiler was short and dapper, with a greasy, swarthy face and long sideboards. He leered at Ava, and said:

'Yeah, beautiful — I know, you wanna be photographed right away. All you dames are the same. I'm busy, come back another night.' He peered at her intently. 'Wait a minute — let's see you in the light. Don't I know you?'

He reached out a thin greasy hand and pulled her into the faint light, staring at her face; 'Jeeze — it's Gail!'

For a minute he could hardly believe his eyes, then he said, roughly:

'Get the hell outa here! Don't you know you're hot? All the cops in New York are looking for you.'

Ava thought it a good idea to let him think she was her sister. She asked, quickly:

'Where can I find Chandos?' The Smiler seemed surprised.

'If you don't know, how can I? You were with him when he bumped Belknap, weren't you? That was a damn stupid thing to do, anyway. Now get outa here — I don't want the cops on my doorstep.'

He looked at her again, admiration in his eyes.

'That's a neat disguise, Gail. You certainly look different without a lot of make-up and wearing simple clothes.' He shook his head. 'But you won't fool the cops none, not with that bronze hair of yours — and wearing Chandos's jewellery too. You oughta have more sense.'

Ava said, desperately:

'Tell me where Chandos is. I've got to find him.'

The Smiler thought about it. Suddenly, his smile widened and he murmured:

'Sure baby, I'll help you. It'll be like old times, you and me . . .'

His hands reached out, grabbed her. Ava struggled as his lips fastened on hers and he slobbered wet kisses over her mouth and face. He released her, growled:

'You've got kinda fussy since you've been running with Chandos. If I didn't have a dame inside . . . never mind, there'll be plenty of time if you beat this dragnet. Your pics still sell like hotcakes, Gail — any time you want to come back in the business, it's okay with me. I was thinking of moving out to the west coast. Maybe I'll see you out there, huh?'

Ava reminded him: 'Chandos's hide-out?'

'Oh, yeah.' He thought about it. 'I guess the only place he can go is the 59th Avenue address. That fat bitch Popocopolis bought it through me. It's a redstone bungalow with a 'To Let' sign outside.

How come you don't know about it?'

Ava said: 'We separated. Now I've nowhere to hide.'

Her answer allayed The Smiler's suspicions.

'Yeah. I guess you'll find him there. Don't forget what I said about the west coast, Gail — if you beat this rap.'

Abruptly, he shut the door in her face, leaving Ava in the darkness of the area porch. She went up the steps to the cab and said:

'Take me to a telephone booth.'

The driver started the cab, turned into Franklin Avenue. Ava shuddered as she remembered The Smiler's familiarity; surely Gail could not have had more than a business arrangement with such a man?

If she'd known the sort of men Gail had met since she moved to New York, she'd have come to take her home long ago. Ava blamed herself for her sister's trouble — somehow she had to help her. She prayed that it was not too late.

The cab stopped outside a drugstore on Franklin Avenue and Ava went inside to make her call. There was only one booth and that was in use. A pimply-faced youth in short, tight-fitting slacks, yellow socks and striped sweat shirt was chewing gum and shooting a line to a cute little number at the other end of the line. Ava fretted, waiting for him to finish with the 'phone.

When, after anxious minutes for Ava, he came out he said:

'Hiya, toots, how about a date?'

Ava moved past him, ignoring the way he looked at her. She closed the door of the 'phone booth and inserted coins, dialling the number of Johnny Fortune's apartment. The bell rang insistently for several minutes, but there was no answer. Johnny was not at home.

She replaced the receiver with a feeling of helplessness. Johnny had promised to help her and now he was out; she didn't know what to do. If she went to 59th Avenue and found Gail, her sister would be with the gang. Ava daren't go to the police — Johnny was the only one who could help. If only . . .

Aya made up her mind. Her sister was in trouble, needed her. She'd go to 59th

Avenue and try to get Gail away from the gang, smuggle her out of New York somehow. She didn't know how she'd do it; the whole thing seemed impossible — but she had to help her young sister. That was all that mattered.

She went back to the cab, and told the driver:

'I want to go to Queen's College — and hurry please.'

A map told her the College was not far from 59th Avenue; she'd walk from there, not wishing to attract attention to the house where Gail was hiding. The cab went up Greenpoint Avenue, past Calvary Cemetery to Queens Boulevard; east to the Horace Harding Boulevard, crossing Connecting Highway.

She was deep in the Queens area of New York now and there were police everywhere. Whole blocks were being cordoned and searched; traffic was held up and it was only the cab driver's instinctive dislike of officialdom that got her through without questioning. Several times, the driver took his cab on detours to avoid the dragnet. They passed through

Flushing Meadow and stopped on Kissena Boulevard, outside the College.

Ava paid off the cab, waited for it to get out of sight then left the shadow of the College walls. She moved quickly along the sidewalk, turned down 164th Street to the North Hempstead Turnpike and found herself between St. Mary's Cemetery and the Kissena Park golf course.

There were few people about in this section and the moonlight was bright on the green of the course and the white gravestones in the cemetery. Ava walked down 167th to 59th Avenue — and found the redstone bungalow.

The house was in darkness; the weed-strewn garden and 'To Let' sign gave it a deserted appearance. Ava's heart sank; suppose The Smiler had been lying and she'd come on a wild goose chase? She told herself this was just the sort of derelict house a gang on the run would use.

She went round the side of the house and found the garage. Giant elms overhung the walls of the cemetery; it was eerie and lonely and Ava's heart thumped wildly. The windows at the back were covered; no chink of light showed anywhere. She hammered the back door with her fist . . .

The door opened suddenly and a pair of massive black hands caught her by the throat and dragged her into the dark interior.

★   ★   ★

The afternoon passed quickly. Johnny Fortune stayed with the police, hoping to get a lead on Gail Gray. Since the discovery of the empty cellar on Silver Bar, they had found the escape boat tied up at the pier on 165th. The dead mechanic at the garage chalked up another crime to Chandos; investigations showed that a black saloon had been used for the getaway. Reports came in; the car had been seen heading north.

Conflicting rumours gave the D.A. and Lieutenant Dix a headache. The car had been seen in so many places at the same time, by people only too willing to help, that it soon became clear that the gang had gone to earth somewhere. The police dragnet widened covering a larger area.

Dix said, with a certain grimness: 'They can't get out of Queens. All roads, railroad stations and airports are guarded. Launches watch the coast. It's only a matter of time before we find the hideout.'

Johnny stayed on to watch the police operate. Dix still seemed suspicious and Johnny barely had time to slip away for one 'phone call to Ava, to let her know her sister was still loose. Block by block, the dragnet worked across the city; police closed off each area, searching houses, questioning everyone. Walkie-talkie radio kept the D.A. in touch with his men. It had the atmosphere of a wartime operation, the pace set by the impatient Thad Belknap.

Evening brought a cooling breeze and dark shadows — and the search went on by moonlight. To the excited and bewildered inhabitants of Queens, it seemed that all New York's police force was stationed in that area. Uniformed cops and plainclothes detectives, grim-faced and carrying guns, closed in, section by section, tightening the net about the Chandos gang. The cordon narrowed the gap between their quarry; there could be no escape. The dragnet moved to an inevitable close — the fight to take the killers of Roy Belknap.

Still Thad Belknap was not satisfied. He turned to the D.A., cold eyes glittering, and said:

'I'm going to broadcast again. I'll increase the reward for the location of Chandos's hideout. Someone must know where they are — some crook will sell them out if I make it worth his while.'

A police car drove him to the radio station. Johnny Fortune looked at Dix.

'I'll leave you boys to it — time I had some shut-eye. Let me know when you find them, I want to be in at the kill.'

Dix said: 'Yeah, we'll let you know. And keep your nose clean, Johnny — if you learn anything, don't try keeping it to yourself. Belknap and the D.A. will bust you wide open if you try to pull any fancy stuff.'

Johnny grinned. 'I'll be good!'

He drove his coupé to a 'phone booth and dialled Ava's hotel number. It was late, but he knew she would be up, waiting for news of her sister. He heard the 'phone bell buzzing at the other end; Ava didn't answer.

Johnny listened for several minutes, fretting. Then he went back to his car and drove towards Manhattan. Something must have happened to Ava and he intended to find out what.

Twice he was stopped by police patrols; the first time at the junction of Interborough and Woodhaven Boulevard; then again at the Queensborough Bridge, where every car was being checked before crossing the East River. On Manhattan, he went along East 60th Street and down Third Avenue.

Arriving at the Courtfield Hotel, he slipped past the clerk at the desk and used the stairway to reach Ava's apartment. He rang, tried the door — locked. There was no one in the passage; Johnny used a piece of steel wire to open the lock. He went inside, moving quickly from room to room.

She was out, and that brought a frown to Johnny's face. Then he found her note, saying she'd gone to see The Smiler. Johnny swore softly; he knew The Smiler's reputation and the thought of him laying hands on Ava made his blood hot. He left the hotel in a hurry, driving back over Queensborough, onto Long Island.

The coupé travelled south down Vernon Boulevard, crossed Newtown Creek to Greenpoint. It didn't take Johnny long to find 7b India Street. He went down the dark area steps and tried the door; the handle turned, but it was bolted on the inside. He rang the bell and waited.

Johnny Fortune tensed as he heard the sound of a bolt being withdrawn. At the first sign of light from the gloom, he hit the door with his shoulder, crashing it wide open. The Smiler staggered back, swearing profusely. Johnny hit him in the face, three times in quick succession, and grabbed his wrists with one hand; his other hand took the gun from The Smiler's pocket.

Johnny said: 'All right. We'll go inside, Smiler — and no tricks. You and I are going to have a heart-to-heart talk.'

At the end of the passage, bright light showed behind a curtain. Johnny pushed The Smiler ahead of him, into the studio. The only piece of furniture in the room was a divan. Round it were grouped cameras and lights. The walls were adorned by photographs of glamour girls.

There was a girl in the studio, posing in high-heeled shoes. She looked at The Smiler's face, bloody where Johnny had hit him, and said:

'I don't want any trouble. I'm getting outa here.'

Johnny grinned at her.

'Beat it, luscious,' he said. 'I've business with The Smiler.'

The girl grabbed her fur coat and ran from the room. He hit the Smiler again, knocking him across the divan. He stood over The Smiler, looking down at the man. The Smiler no longer looked dapper with a smear of blood across his greasy face; his teeth still showed, but the smile was forced.

Johnny said: 'A girl came here this evening. Not long ago. Where is she?'

The Smiler bared his teeth, wriggling into a sitting position. His voice was flat:

'I don't know what you're talking about. You're crazy if you think — '

Johnny hit him again, across the face with the butt of The Smiler's own gun. The Smiler whimpered:

'Don't — don't — '

Johnny laughed, but there was no humour in the sound. His blue eyes had a steely glint and his slim body was taut with raging fury.

'She wanted to know where she could find Chandos — remember?'

The Smiler said: 'You mean Gail? Why didn't you say so? You a friend of Chandos?'

He had a hopeful note in his voice. Johnny destroyed that hope. He knocked The Smiler flat again. Johnny thought it was cute of Ava to let him think she was Gail — but he was prepared to use more violent methods to get the information he wanted. He said:

'So you told her where to find

Chandos? Well now you're going to tell me!'

'Like hell I am!' The Smiler shouted, and hurled himself at Johnny.

Johnny clubbed him with the gun butt. He was in no mood to play games with Ava walking in on Chandos; he wanted that address in a hurry. He slashed The Smiler across the throat with the edge of his flat hand, half-choking him.

'You're going to give me Chandos's address or I'm going to leave you in no condition to talk again. Where did you tell the girl to go?'

The Smiler was scared now. He looked at Johnny with pleading in his eyes.

'I can't tell you — I can't. Chandos would kill me . . . '

Johnny laughed and hit him some more. He grated:

'Chandos isn't here — and I am. And I'll kill you if you don't talk.'

The Smiler tried to get away, sliding over the divan. Johnny followed him, driving him into a corner. He'd dropped the gun now and was using his fists, driving short jabs hard and fast to The

Smiler's belly and face.

'I don't mind beating you to a pulp,' Johnny said grimly. 'In fact, I'd enjoy it. I'll go on hitting you till you tell me where to find Chandos.'

The Smiler sagged under Johnny's punches. He tried to raise his arms in defence, but Johnny battered them down. The Smiler was in a bad way; he made one desperate attempt to get clear. Johnny moved back; got his arms round The Smiler's waist and lifted him in the air. He threw him across the room. The Smiler hit the far wall and crumpled.

Johnny threw water in The Smiler's face, kicked him around.

'Chandos's address — or I'll finish you, Smiler,' he said coldly.

The Smiler couldn't take any more. He wiped blood from his mouth, gasping:

'All right, I'll talk. For God's sake, don't hit me again.'

Johnny said: 'I'm listening.'

The Smiler said: 'He's got a redstone bungalow on 59th Avenue. You'll know it by the 'To Let' sign outside. Don't tell Chandos I squealed — '

Johnny Fortune turned away, ignoring The Smiler; he didn't care what happened to the swarthy man. He was thinking of Ava, alone, going to visit Chandos and Madame Popocopolis, and his blood turned to ice at the thought.

He went outside to his coupé and drove furiously eastwards. If he'd known it, he used almost the same route that Ava had, earlier that night; along Queens Boulevard and through Flushing Meadow. He turned down 166th Street to 59th Avenue and watched for the redstone bungalow.

He saw it almost at once, lying back under the shadow of the giant elms that overhung the walls of St. Mary's Cemetery — and drove past, parking his car out of sight. Johnny returned to the house on foot taking advantage of every piece of cover, keeping to the shadows. There was no light and no sound from the house; nothing to indicate whether or not Ava was inside.

He contemplated calling in the cops and surrounding the bungalow; he'd stopped worrying about Gail — she'd have to take her chances with the rest of the gang. But if Ava was inside, a prisoner, Johnny couldn't take the risk of the gang using her as hostage. He had to be sure she was safe before bringing Dix and his men on the scene.

He circled the house, looking for a way in. A back upstairs window caught his eye. He climbed the cemetery wall, moved out along the branch of an elm, his swordstick clenched between his teeth. He reached the window and tried it. The catch was fastened on the inside, but that didn't worry Johnny Fortune.

He twisted the handle of his cane and a thin steel blade shot out. Jamming the blade between the centre frames of the casement, he forced back the catch and opened the window. He climbed through and dropped to the passage, listening.

The upper hall of the house was deserted and in darkness. He felt his way to the top of the stairs.

Voices drifted up to him. He recognized Madame Popocopolis's voice — and Ava's.

Quietly, he descended the stairs, light blue eyes gleaming with excitement. Again, Johnny Fortune was the debonair adventurer about to rescue a damsel in distress.

9

Ava Gray choked as giant hands gripped her throat. The door closed behind her, blocking off the moonlight, and she was in total darkness with her assailant. She felt herself lifted bodily in the air and carried along a passage. Through a door was a lighted room, and she was released.

Ava gasped for air, holding her neck where thumb marks darkened her white skin. It was some seconds before she recovered sufficiently to look at the people in the room. The first person she saw was Nugent.

She knew his name by the description that had been broadcast over the radio — and there could be no mistaking the giant negro.

He stood seven feet high. The check sports coat he wore clashed with green gaberdine slacks; the hand-painted colours on his tie showed clearly against the backdrop of a crimson shirt. He stood on thick crepe-soled shoes, grinning at her, his tiny eyes bright, massive hands opening and closing in a menacing gesture.

'Yo be quiet, missy, an' mebbe I no hurt yo. Ah ain't one to hurt a lady.'

Ava looked past him. She recognized Harvey Chandos and Snowy; she'd seen them before, at Belmont Park. Chandos sucked the end of a cigar, his eyes cold in a red, blotchy face. Snowy wasn't wearing his cloth cap, but his drape suit still looked oddly out of place with the cheap striped shirt he wore. His bowed legs, shock of hair and wild eyes made him look even more stunted than he was. He didn't say anything, but a nerve twitched in his face.

A cackle of laughter made Ava shudder. She turned to look into the bright, piggy eyes of Madame Popocopolis. The fat woman was old and ugly and wore a soiled dress of black velvet; her rolls of fat quivered as she laughed and her double chins moved in speech. Her voice was strangely firm.

'So you're Gail's sister, dearie? And

you want to take Gail home and reform her bad ways?'

She cackled with laughter again, her whole grotesque shape rocking back and forth till the chair creaked under her.

'Tell her you're glad to see your sister, Gail!'

Ava saw her sister then, and it was a shock. Her eyes opened wider as she saw Gail sprawled in a chair, cigarette smouldering in the long black jade holder clenched lightly between her teeth. Gail had a tumbler of gin in her hand. She removed the cigarette holder, laughed harshly, and said:

'To a family reunion!'

She poured the gin down her throat and threw the empty glass at Ava. Her voice held a note of mockery, jeering:

'Help yourself — no one here minds whether a girl drinks or not.'

Ava's eyes watered. She looked at her sister, trying to conceal the horror and pity she felt. It seemed incredible that the woman she saw was her kid sister, four years younger than herself. The maroon evening dress, low cut with bare shoulders, the way she showed her silk-clad legs, the mask of thickly applied make-up, made her appear much older; Gail had lost the charm of youth. Ava fought for self-control, blaming herself for what had happened to Gail.

She said: 'Gail, the police are looking for you — the whole city is being combed. You must let me take you away from here before it's too late.'

Gail Gray laughed; it was a harsh, brutal sound. Her brown eyes, gold flecks swirling angrily, were cold as ice.

'Tell me something I don't know, sis. I'm staying here, with Chandos, where I'm safe. You aren't handing me to the cops on a plate.'

Ava pleaded: 'I don't want the police to get you, Gail, I want to help you escape. That's why I stayed in New York, to help you. Johnny Fortune's helping me — he'll see you get out of the country. Won't you leave these people while there is still time?'

Madame Popocopolis hissed: 'So Johnny Fortune is still interfering in my business? I'll attend to that young man in due course.' Her piggy eyes fixed on Ava. 'And dearie, what makes you think I'd let you walk out of here with Gail? Even if she wanted to leave — which she doesn't.'

Harvey Chandos lit a fresh cigar, scowling. He said:

'What I want to know is: how did she find us?'

The fat woman leered at Ava.

'Yes, tell us, dearie — we're all friends here. We don't want to keep secrets, do we?' She cackled with laughter.

Ava said: 'The Smiler told me — '

Snowy swore virulently; his eyes grew wilder.

'The Smiler! The dirty double-crosser — I'll pump him full o' lead, see if I don't.'

Ava shuddered. Madame Popocopolis said:

'That's a good idea, Snowy, but it may be too late. We should have taken care of The Smiler a long time ago. I knew that rat wasn't to be trusted.'

Ava didn't like The Smiler, but she had to say something to save him. If Snowy killed him, she felt that his blood would

137

be on her hands.

'He didn't double-cross you,' she said. 'He thought I was Gail.'

Ava's sister laughed.

'The fool! Fancy mistaking a stuck-up prude like you — for me. The Smiler's losing his touch with women!'

She stubbed out her cigarette, rose from her chair and walked towards Ava. Her hips swayed. She struck Ava across the face, jeering:

'You're finished, sis — you won't get out of here alive. And you won't bother me again. I'm glad you're going to die — glad!'

Ava's face went white. She felt numbed with horror; this was so unlike the reunion she'd imagined.

Gail didn't want her help, she wanted to live with these horrible people. Something had happened to her sister, changed her. Ava knew now that she was all bad, beyond saving. Tears formed in her eyes, rolled down her cheeks.

Madame Popocopolis said:

'This alters things. If Gail's sister found us, Johnny Fortune can — and the cops.

We've got to change our plans.'

Chandos stared at Ava over the glowing tip of his cigar.

'Maybe she'll be of use to us. We'll give them her as a decoy. She's enough like Gail to pass — as a corpse. It'll take their minds off us for the get-away.'

Gail said, eagerly: 'Let me kill her. I've always loathed the way she tried to run my life. I'll enjoy doing it.'

The fat woman moved in her chair. Her double chins quivered in speech.

'It's an idea, Harvey, certainly it is.' She brooded on it, then said: 'But there's something to be done first. The D.A.'s under pressure from Thad Belknap — if we can kill him, the cops will ease off. Then, if we give them Ava's body, they'll be satisfied — it'll give us the chance we want to escape the dragnet.'

Chandos's face lit up.

'That's good — good. But we've got to work fast. There isn't much time.'

Madame Popocopolis looked at Snowy. His face twitched; he knew what was coming and he wasn't keen on the job. The cops were all over the streets and it wouldn't be easy to get near Belknap. He licked his lips in apprehension.

'Get after him now. Use your gun and don't make any mistakes. It might be an idea to kill The Smiler at the same time. Get going.'

Snowy pulled his cap over his shock of hair. He checked his gun. Without speaking, he went out of the room, out of the house. No one argued with Madame Popocopolis. He wasn't feeling good about this job — but he'd sooner face all the cops in New York City than go against the fat woman.

Ava made one final attempt to save her sister.

'Gail, let me take you away from here. You haven't a chance of escaping with these people. I want to help you — let me — '

Gail laughed wildly. She slapped Ava across the face twice, bringing a flush to her white cheeks. Ava stood still; she couldn't fight her sister. Gail tore the ruby-studded necklace from Ava's throat, pulled the bracelet off her wrist.

'They're mine,' she said savagely,

'mine! I don't know how you got them, but they're mine. Harvey gave them to me, and now, I'll take them back — you won't need them in the morgue!'

Her laughter was hysterical. She turned to Chandos, said: 'Give me a gun — I'll do it now.'

The fat woman snapped: 'You crazy fool — I won't have any shooting here. I'll let you kill her, but you'll use a knife. A knife doesn't make any noise.'

Ava stared at her sister with horror, hardly able to believe her eyes; she saw Gail, crazy with blood-lust; heard her say:

'A knife — give me a knife!'

Madame Popocopolis watched Gail with a sneer on her ugly face. She said:

'Later. Not now, Gail. We don't want a dead body on our hands till it's time to use it. And maybe Johnny Fortune will be around — I guess he's keen on your sister or he wouldn't be running around in circles trying to help you. She'll make nice bait to catch him.'

Her piggy eyes bored into the painted mask of Gail Gray's face and she smirked at her thoughts. Ava would have to die — she took that for granted. But maybe it would really be Gail's body she used to hold up the police search — it was time she got rid of her. Gail had too much hold over Harvey; she was dangerous . . .

Ava looked wildly from her sister to Madame Popocopolis, from Chandos to Nugent. A low, choked sob broke from her lips; it seemed she must wake up from this nightmare — it couldn't be real, this cold, calculated discussion of her death, as if she weren't there at all. She couldn't bring herself to believe that people could act this way.

Gail glared at Madame Popocopolis, frustrated in her desire to kill her sister. Hatred boiled inside her. God, how she hated the fat bitch! She thought: I'll kill her when I finish Ava — then Harvey and I will get clear, over the border to start a new life together.

Chandos turned on Ava, who was still sobbing, and struck her viciously.

'Stop that snivelling!' he grated.

Nugent grinned, showing gleaming

white teeth in a black face. His hands opened and closed significantly.

'Yo wan' me to quiet her, Chan?'

Ava backed away, face white and drawn. She looked wildly around for a way of escape. Her eyes saw the inner door slowly open . . . and Johnny Fortune appeared. She should have kept quiet, drawn attention from the door to give him a chance to act — but she was too upset, too frightened.

She flung herself across the room, into his arms, crying:

'Johnny! Oh, Johnny — take me away from here.'

Madame Popocopolis hissed:

'Nugent — take him!'

The giant lumbered towards the door, arms swinging. Johnny Fortune was hampered with Ava clinging to him. He pushed her away, tried to bring up his swordcane. Nugent hit the girl across the back of the neck, felling her where she stood. Ava crumpled to the ground without a murmur and Johnny, moving forward, tripped over her body.

Nugent caught his arm, tore the cane

from his hand and threw it across the room. Gail panted eagerly:

'Kill him, Nugent — kill him!'

The giant was doing his best. He held Johnny with one hand, dangling him like a puppet at arm's length while he pounded his face with his other fist. Johnny broke free, face gashed and bleeding, one eye closed. He was wild with fury at the way Ava had been treated; he came in, throwing terrific punches to Nugent's stomach, driving him back.

Johnny knew he had to finish Nugent fast if he were to do any good. He still had Chandos and the two women to take care of before he could help Ava.

He smashed his fists in quick succession to Nugent's jaw. It felt as if he hit concrete. The giant rocked, went back on his heels, but Johnny's punches only shook him. He swung a right hook to Johnny's head.

Johnny Fortune saw it coming and knew this punch was the end of the fight. He couldn't get out of the way in time. Couldn't even roll his head to lessen the force. He had one glimpse of a grinning black face — then a steam-hammer hit him and he went under.

There was blackness.

10

Snowy went through the iron gate into the cemetery, back of the bungalow on 59th Avenue. The moonlight was bright on ghostly white gravestones, casting long black shadows from the elms. Snowy travelled fast and silent, keeping in shadow, hiding at the least sound or movement.

He knew he was taking the biggest risk of his life; to reach Thad Belknap, he had to break through the police cordon — but he'd sooner do that than risk displeasing Madame Popocopolis. He'd seen her deal with people she no longer trusted; he shivered at the thought.

Beyond the cemetery, he cut down dimly lit side streets, moving south. The cops would be working their way north from Jamaica Bay and Thad Belknap would be with them. Snowy went to meet the dragnet. He crossed the grounds of the Pomonak Country Club and came

146

out on 160th Street, kept going till he reached the hospital at the junction of Grand Central Parkway and Parsons Boulevard.

He paused in the shadow of the hospital grounds, listening. The cops were moving up Parsons — and Belknap would be with them. He only had to wait . . .

He selected a patch of shadow cast by trees in front of the hospital. There was a smooth lawn and a statue of a white horse, head up, mane tossing. Snowy grinned at the idea that came to him. He had been a jockey, hadn't he? Well, this was one horse that wouldn't throw him.

He moved quickly to the statue, climbed the pedestal and mounted the horse's back. The stonework was cold but Snowy didn't let that worry him; he'd found the perfect hiding place. The statue was in shadow — and who was going to look at a stone horse anyway? No one would notice that the rider was flesh and blood. The sheer daring of his move would cover him.

He sat motionless, staring beyond the stone ears of the horse, listening for the cops. He heard them move nearer. One hand slid into his pocket, pulled out a paper package. He unfolded the paper, took the white powder between thumb and forefinger, raised it to his nostrils and inhaled. The empty paper fluttered to the ground.

The dope quietened the nervous twitch in Snowy's face. His eyes dulled and the skin grew taut about his mouth. His body went rigid. He pulled his gun from its holster and held it flat against the horse's neck, waiting for Thad Belknap to appear.

The dragnet moved up Parsons Boulevard. Cops passed Snowy without noticing him. They searched the hospital grounds and went on. He was right inside the cordon now — cops were all round him. Then he saw the D.A. and Dix come up the street; Belknap was right behind them, a gaunt figure with the moonlight shining on his bald head. Snowy tensed, waiting for him to draw level with the statue; the gun was dead weight in his hand.

Belknap walked into range. Snowy raised his gun, slowly, edging it over the horse's mane, resting it on the stonework. A police car drove up, siren screaming for attention. The car stopped beside the D.A., and two cops and a man with a swarthy face got out.

A cop said: 'This guy says he knows where the gang's hiding. He'll only talk to Belknap.'

Snowy cursed under his breath, recognizing The Smiler; the rat was double-crossing them. His gun shifted, from Belknap to the Smiler. Lieutenant Dix, hat brim upturned, spectacles glinting in the moonlight, looked at The Smiler.

'This is Belknap,' he said coldly. 'You can spill it, Smiler.'

Belknap said: 'What do you know?'

The Smiler was in no hurry. His teeth showed and his eyes shifted from the cops to Thad Belknap. His voice had a whine to it.

'You're paying a quarter of a million bucks? That right?'

Belknap nodded briskly.

'You'll be paid — if you lead us to Chandos and the girl.'

The D.A. snorted. His dark close-cropped hair seemed to stand up. His voice was hard.

'Talk, Smiler — or we'll take you inside and use rubber hose to get it out of you. I've no time for double-crossers.'

Neither had Snowy. But he was torn between two targets, Thad Belknap and The Smiler. Inevitably, his aim suffered. Even as he pulled the trigger, he knew he'd missed — the slug tore between the two men and they dived for cover. Snowy had no time for a second shot — cops were all round him.

A barrage of crossfire smashed against the stone horse. Snowy felt hot lead tear at his body. He slipped sideways, felt himself falling. Even then the cops didn't stop shooting — bullets whined and crashed through the night air, filling the street with cordite fumes. A dozen slugs buried themselves in Snowy before he hit the ground; but he didn't feel his head touch the grass — he was dead halfway to the ground.

Dix turned the body over with his foot.

'It's Snowy,' he said. 'The first of the

gang has paid for Roy Belknap's killing.' He shouted at cops: 'Search around — maybe the others are here.'

But the dragnet found no one. Belknap's face lit up with a grim light.

'The first one — now for the rest of the gang.' He turned on The Smiler. 'Where are they? Hurry man, if they get away, you won't be paid. I'm paying only if you deliver them into my hands.'

The Smiler was trembling. Snowy's slug had come near enough to break his nerve. He wasn't sure that Chandos and Madame Popocopolis weren't hiding nearby, and that thought nearly gave him heart failure. Gone was all thought of Belknap's reward money — all he wanted was to get clear. He must have been crazy to think he could double-cross the fat woman and get away with it.

Dix grabbed The Smiler by his shoulders and shook him like a puppy. He slapped his face hard. His voice grated:

'Talk, you rat — talk!'

The Smiler looked round at the ring of coppers. He saw hard faces, pitiless. He talked:

'59th Avenue — a redstone bungalow with a 'To Let' sign outside.'

Dix snapped orders. Cars moved off at high speed travelling north. The D.A. snapped:

'That had better be right, Smiler. If Chandos gets away, we ain't gonna like you. Neither will Chandos.'

The Smiler gulped. He, too, could see it was to his advantage that the gang were caught; he'd gone too far to back out now.

'There's a back way through St. Mary's Cemetery,' he said. 'They'll use that if they're cornered.'

Dix said: 'Not now they won't!'

Belknap and the D.A., with the lieutenant, piled into a police car. The driver stepped on the accelerator and Dix spoke into the radio mike.

'All cars proceed towards 59th Avenue. Cordon St. Mary's Cemetery and area contained by Horace Harding Boulevard, 164th Street, North Hempstead Turnpike and Fresh Meadow Lane. That's all!'

★ ★ ★

The room was small and dimly lit. From a distance, behind a closed door, came the murmur of voices. His head ached and dried blood cracked as his lips opened in a groan and air wheezed into his lungs. The dull pain in the centre of his face could only be his nose. One eye wouldn't open properly, but Johnny Fortune could see enough to worry him.

Ava Gray lay on the floor, arms and legs tightly tied, a gag in her mouth. She was conscious and wriggled around to prove it, smiling at him with her soft brown eyes. Johnny began to remember things more clearly — the fight with Nugent ending with that terrific punch.

That told him why they'd only tied his hands and hadn't bothered with a gag. They hadn't expected him to recover consciousness so quickly. Johnny tested the bonds about his wrists by straining at them; they gave a little, but not enough to matter. He wasn't going to get loose before someone came to finish him off.

Sure, he could shout for help — but would there be anyone to hear? It was certain they'd hear in the next room

— and both he and Ava would die instantly. Johnny shook his head; somehow, he had to get free — and quick. That was the only hope.

He rolled over, looking round the room — and nearly laughed. Someone had thrown his cane into a corner; they hadn't known the cane held a sharp steel blade. Johnny wriggled towards it. Ava watched him, puzzled.

Johnny called, softly: 'Don't worry, Ava — I'll soon have you out of this.'

He was glad his hands were tied in front of him; that way, he could see what he was doing. He got his hands round the cane handle, twisted — the steel blade shot out, glittering in the dim light.

Ava's eyes shone as she saw what he was doing; her heart thumped and she began to hope again. But could Johnny cut himself free before Chandos or someone came through from the other room? She rolled across the floor, pressing her body against the door. She wouldn't stop them long, but she might hold the door shut long enough to give Johnny a few extra seconds — and seconds could count now.

Johnny wedged the shaft of the swordstick between his knees and got his wrists over the blade. Slowly, he began to work his hands to and fro, sawing at the ropes. The sword slipped and cut his wrist; blood ran over his hands, making them slippery, more difficult to work with. He cursed, got the blade into a fresh position and started again.

Voices were raised in the other room. An argument was going on. Johnny heard Gail speak, then Madame Popocopolis; he couldn't distinguish words but it sounded as if they were quarrelling. He worked faster, sweating, knowing time was short.

A strand of rope parted; he strained his arms in a useless effort to break free, used the sword blade again. He kept nicking his wrists till they were sore with tiny cuts and his hands were covered in blood. All the time, the voices in the other room rose in anger.

Another strand snapped. The cane slipped again. Johnny swore bitterly, wriggled round, got the sword wedged between his knees and attacked his bonds with fresh vigour. Something told him he hadn't much time. He jammed the blade between his hands and sawed furiously. He lost a lot of skin and blood, but the ropes gave. With one wrench of his arms, he broke the last strand.

Johnny came to his feet in a hurry. Someone started to scream in the next room. The sound was choked off in mid-voice and something hit the floor with a flat thud. The voices stopped. Johnny wiped blood off his hands and grabbed the sword; he crossed the room to Ava, bent over her and cut her cords.

She tore the gag from her mouth, sobbing with relief.

Johnny caught her in his arms, kissed her. The way she clung to him, he wanted to go on holding her like that for the rest of his life; but there were things to do. Something had happened in the next room and he wanted to know what. He pushed Ava against the wall, grasped the sword-stick tighter. His light blue eyes glinted and he smiled grimly.

Then the door opened and Nugent came into the room.

★   ★   ★

Harvey Chandos and Nugent came back from the small room, after tying up Johnny Fortune and the girl, to find the two women glaring at one another with hatred in their eyes and murder in their hearts.

Nugent moved to one side, silent; the giant wasn't bothered by tension — as long as someone gave him orders, he was happy.

Chandos felt uneasy. He'd seen this trouble coming for a long time. Madame Popocopolis never had liked him playing around with dames, though she usually hid her jealousy; it was Gail's fault for deliberately causing trouble. He lit a cigar, scowling at them; now was a fine time for a showdown!

He watched Gail closely. Her lips were tight, face pale; only the slight trembling of her body, the blazing light in her eyes showed her emotion. Sure, she was a good-looking dame — but there were plenty like her. He sighed a little; it seemed a shame she would have to die soon.

The fat woman stirred in her chair, smiling to herself, looking from Gail to Chandos; her piggy eyes told him she'd already decided about Gail. He'd seen that look on other occasions, just before other girls who'd kept him happy had died. Glamour girls came and went in Harvey Chandos's life — but Madame Popocopolis went on for ever. Or so it seemed . . .

Not that Chandos had any liking for the fat woman; he, too, hated her hold over him. He'd much rather have killed her and kept Gail — but Madame Popocopolis had the brains of the outfit, and he knew it. Without her, he'd be sunk. So it was Gail who must die.

Madame Popocopolis's double chins moved. She said:

'I've decided that Gail's sister isn't enough to throw the cops off our trail. We'll use Gail instead.'

The firmness of her tone upset Gail.

She shivered with fear, appealed to Chandos.

'Harvey — don't listen to her. We two can get away — you want me, don't you?'

She swayed towards him, smiling provocatively, using all her charm to get him on her side. She said, softly:

'Kill this fat bitch for me, Harvey — I want you to myself.'

Madame Popocopolis cackled with laughter. Her grotesque body shook, rolls of fat quivering.

'Poor Gail — she thinks she means more to you than me. Show her, Harvey.' Her voice was suddenly shrill, cold and hard. 'Show her how much she means to you. Kill her, Harvey!'

Chandos looked from one to the other, and looked away. He was unable to face the burning hatred in their eyes; he felt sick — but he knew what he must do. His voice was thick.

'Nugent — '

He broke off, watching the two women, shuddering. The cigar tasted foul in his mouth; he threw it to the floor, stamped on it. His tone became harsh.

'Nugent — *Gail*!'

The giant moved forward, his black face split in a horrible grin, hands opening and closing.

'Sho, boss — Ah takes care o' her. She won't be no trouble to mah, no trouble at all.'

Gail shivered. Her voice crept out from between painted lips, lips that were strangely bright in her pale face.

'Harvey! Her, *her* — not me!'

Chandos looked away, not speaking. Gail, so far as he was concerned, was already dead. The fat woman jeered:

'So much for your power over Harvey, dearie. Now you know the truth about men. You see, there are other young girls for them to play with — but not so many brains!'

Gail whirled on her, screaming:

'You fat bitch! I'll get you — I'll finish you myself!' She dodged Nugent's outstretched hands, hurled herself at Madame Popocopolis. Her fingernails clawed the wrinkled skin, gouging deeply. She got her hands wound into the fat woman's grey hair, jerked her head back.

Words slobbered out of Madame Popocopolis's mouth as her ugly face became
contorted with fear and pain.

'Nugent, you black — ! Get her off'n
me. Choke her with those great hands of
yours!'

The giant lunged forward. His hands
went round Gail's slim neck, fastening
like a vice. The muscles of his arms
bulged as his grip tightened. Gail gasped,
but her hands never left the fat woman;
she knew she was going to die, that she
couldn't keep off the giant — and she was
determined to take Madame Popocopolis
with her.

Black hands throttled her, choking off
the air from her lungs. Her heart
pounded; her face turned purple — a
buzzing sounded in her ears and still she
dragged on the fat woman's hair, hands
clenched in fury. A black film slid over
her eyes; the strength went out of her
arms and her hands dropped slack.

Madame Popocopolis came out of the
chair with blazing eyes and quivering
chins. Gail's attack had upset her more
than she liked to admit. She fought for

self-control, gasping and wheezing, as she watched Nugent strangle the girl who'd tried to kill her.

Nugent stood with his feet wide apart, dangling Gail's limp body in front of him. His hands tightened about her neck till the veins stood out from his black skin. He held her like that till life ceased to flow through Gail's young body; then he dropped her on the floor and stood back, still grinning.

Gail had learnt it doesn't pay to throw in with a tough mob, but the lesson had come too late for her to profit by it. The fat woman cackled, and said:

'Fortune — and Gail's sister. Kill them, Nugent!'

11

Thad Belknap was impatient. He fumed: 'Let's get going — I want the killers of my son.'

The D.A. tried to soothe him. He said; 'Dix is right — it would be a mistake to move too soon. When all our men are in position, then we'll take them. Now we've got the gang bottled up we don't want them to break through.'

Dix pushed his hat back and up. He had lost his owlish expression. Through the cemetery, moonlight was bright on tombstones and the wall at the back; he could just make out the form of the redstone bungalow in the shadow of the elms.

'Yeah, we'll wait a little,' he said, and took the walkie-talkie from the cop behind.

He listened as reports came in:

'Gooch, at the corner of 164th and Turnpike. My men are ready, spread out in single file.'

'Jameson, here. The Horace Harding Boulevard is covered. All set for action.'

'Thomas and section reporting from Fresh Meadow Lane. Not even a ghost could slip by us.' There was a grim chuckle from the walkie-talkie.

Dix said, into the mike:

'All right, let's go. Close in on the bungalow and shoot first if you have to shoot. These birds are tough and they won't give up without a fight. Don't take chances and don't let anyone break through your line — repeat, anyone. Cordon the bungalow but don't move in till you hear three short blasts on a whistle.'

He added, as an afterthought: 'Or shooting!'

Dix glanced at the D.A. and Belknap. Wilson looked tired and harassed; he wasn't used to these night raids, but he couldn't get out of it with Belknap worrying him all the time. Thad Belknap looked grim; his face was grey and lined and the cold light in his eyes showed no hint of mercy. He was impatient to get to grips with his son's murderers; implacable in his desire for revenge.

Dix straightened up, pushing the safety catch off his Detective Special. The red stump of the missing finger on his left hand began to itch — a sure sign of trouble. He waved his men forward.

'Keep with us, Smiler,' he warned. 'I want to keep my eyes on you all the time.'

The Smiler scowled; he wasn't feeling enthusiastic about the raid on the bungalow. He'd have preferred not to have made a personal appearance; if anything went wrong, and Madame Popocopolis escaped, his life wouldn't be worth a used postage stamp. He shivered at the thought.

Dix said: 'I wish I knew where Johnny Fortune was — I don't want him getting in my hair at a time like this. He ought to be in bed — but I'll stake next month's salary he's not.'

The D.A. laughed shortly.

'I'll fix Fortune for good if he's mixed up in this business.'

The Smiler thought he saw a chance to hit back at Johnny for the beating he'd given him. He said:

'I guess you'll find Fortune at the bungalow too. He's keen on the girl, Gail — '

Dix swore.

'The crazy fool! If he thinks he can get her away, I'll — '

Belknap said: 'For God's sake, let's get moving.'

He turned to the patrolman behind. 'Give me your gun.'

The cop hesitated. Dix nodded: 'Give it to him.'

Belknap took the gun. He held it as if he knew how to use it and wanted to badly. His knuckles were white round the butt.

They went through the cemetery, between white tombstones that shone under the moon's ghostly beams. The paths were overgrown with weeds; bracken crackled underfoot. A church clock chimed twice in the silence, the echoes lingering on the still night air. Dix felt tensed up inside; he'd been a professional manhunter a long time, but this grim procession through the graveyard got under his skin. He'd be glad when the action started; he wanted something to take his mind off the white marble slabs jutting up from mounds of earth, like grim sentinels waiting to claim their victims.

Dix stopped again when he reached the inside wall. The redstone bungalow was starkly silhouetted by moonlight against the dark sky. Night clouds scurried overhead. The cops spread out along the wall, taut and jittery, waiting for the signal to attack. Dix spoke softly into the walkie-talkie:

'Everyone set?'

Gooch reported: 'Yeah. We're on 59th Avenue, opposite 167th, and can see the bungalow clearly. No sign of life.'

Jameson came in: 'Ready and waitin'. Hurry it up will ya? My men are getting nerve-strain.'

Thomas answered: 'I'm on 59th, at the junction of 169th Street. The bungalow looks fine from here.'

Dix looked at the D.A. Wilson said, in a low voice:

'All set?'

Dix nodded. A strange calm came over him; this was it.

Belknap fidgeted, the gun heavy in his hand. He was muttering to himself and the lines about his mouth grew taut. Beads of sweat stood out on his great dome of a forehead.

The D.A. said, clearly:

'Okay, lieutenant — let's take them!'

Dix put a whistle to his lips and blew three short blasts. The cops moved in for the kill; from all sides they converged on the house in 59th Avenue. The dragnet had reached its climax. Grim-faced, guns at the ready, uniformed patrolmen and plainclothes detectives assaulted the bungalow; there could be no escape for Roy Belknap's killers. At that moment, shots sounded from inside the redstone bungalow.

⋆ ⋆ ⋆

Johnny Fortune was in no mood for playing games. He had Ava to think of, and Chandos was within call. As the giant Nugent came through the door, Johnny lunged with his swordstick. Nugent saw him too late to save himself; he opened his mouth to shout, brought up his hands . . . but the point of Johnny's sword found the hand-painted nude on his tie, sliced through his crimson shirt into his heart.

Nugent knew a moment of searing agony, then a dark mist swamped the killer of Roy Belknap. His legs sagged and the weight of his huge body pulled him clear of the steel blade; he sank to the floor and sprawled in a heap, motionless. Never again were his black hands going to choke the life from anyone; Nugent was a job for the undertaker.

Ava shuddered, her face white, hands trembling. She clung to Johnny, staring horrified at the corpse. Johnny held her tight, caressed her. He said, grimly:

'Don't waste any pity on him, Ava — he'd have killed us without turning a hair. Anyway, he'd have got the electric chair for Belknap's murder — if the police hadn't shot him full of holes first. Come on — we've got to get out of here.'

He stepped over the dead body of Nugent, stared into the room beyond.

Chandos and Madame Popocopolis were listening to the radio — but it was something else that caught Johnny's attention. Gail Gray, stretched out in death on the floor. Hastily, he moved in front of Ava, to block her view; he wanted to protect her from the shock.

Harvey Chandos moved away from the radio, his red face grey, eyes mirroring terror. His voice was a croak:

'The cops have got Snowy — they're closing in on the house!'

Madame Popocopolis turned, calling, 'Nugent — hurry it up.' She saw Johnny Fortune in the doorway, blood dripping from the sword in his hand, Ava crowding behind him. She snarled:

'Harvey; Fortune's loose — get him!'

At that moment, three short blasts sounded on a police whistle. Johnny laughed.

'Too late, Chandos — the dragnet's closing in. You're finished.'

Chandos went for his gun, blasted shots at Johnny Fortune. Johnny pushed Ava back; she tripped over Nugent's body and went sprawling. Johnny ducked, lunged forward at Chandos with his sword. Chandos's slugs passed through the empty space where they had stood, seconds before.

Harvey Chandos dropped his gun and ran; the bloody sword in Johnny's hand, the steely light in his eyes, frightened him. He made the stairs, started upward, with Johnny right behind him. Ava found her sister's body; she knelt over it, tears staining her cheeks, sobbing. Madame Popocopolis made for the back door leading onto the cemetery, as fast as her bulk would allow. She was alone now, frightened and desperate; she rushed from the bungalow into the moonlight.

Chandos was trapped on the balcony at the top of the stairs. Johnny had him cornered, advanced sword in hand. Chandos moaned in fear; he trembled, backing against the wooden rail over the hallway.

'No — no! Fortune, don't — I didn't mean . . . '

His voice trailed into a scream as he felt the balcony rail give way. He grabbed wildly at space, hurtled downwards. He hit the floor and his screaming stopped abruptly. Crumpled in a grotesque heap, neck broken by the fall, Harvey Chandos had paid for his life of crime.

Johnny went down the stairs to Ava, still huddled over the dead body of her sister. Gail's neck was purple-black where Nugent's strong hands had throttled the life out of her; but her face was calm in death, strangely young and innocent. She no longer looked older than she was; just a kid of nineteen who'd got into bad company and couldn't stand the pace.

Johnny hauled Ava to her feet, kissed her gently.

'Perhaps it's best this way,' he said softly, stroking her face, brushing the tears away. 'At least the cops won't bother her.'

Ava clung to him; now that Gail was dead, she felt that Johnny was all she had in the world. She wanted to go right away with him, to forget the horror of this evening. Johnny pushed her away.

'Wait here,' he said grimly. 'There's still the fat woman to take care of.'

He went out through the door, into the

moonlight, towards the cemetery. Gun shots crackled and the smell of cordite was acrid on the night air. Police seemed to be everywhere. Johnny bumped into Lieutenant Dix.

'Madame Popocopolis broke through into the graveyard,' Dix said. 'She's surrounded, can't possibly escape. What happened in the house?'

Johnny told him swiftly.

Dix grunted: 'So there's only the fat woman left. Maybe we'll get some sleep tonight, after all.'

He shouted fresh instructions to his men, and they closed in for the kill. Madame Popocopolis crouched between jutting tombstones, half-hidden by thick ivy. Her lined face was covered with sweat, her piggy eyes bright with fear. She saw Thad Belknap with the cops, The Smiler close at his heels, and bitter anger surged through her. The Smiler had sold her to the cops — well, he wasn't going to live to profit by his double-cross.

Throwing caution aside, she came out from hiding, Chandos's gun in her hand. Moonlight made her appear like a grotesque spectre, fat and old and ugly. She cackled with mad laughter, shouted to The Smiler:

'This is where you get yours, you double-crossing rat!'

The gun in her fat hand belched red flame and hot lead. Slugs tore at The Smiler, twisted him round, slammed him backwards. He dropped in a heap, moaning and foaming a bloody froth at the mouth, writhing and holding his hands over his stomach. He was dying fast.

Cops opened up on Madame Popocopolis, but she was too quick for them; she ducked for cover. Johnny and Dix stooped over The Smiler. His greasy face was damp with a cold sweat and his mouth twisted into a toothy smile; the lecherous light had gone out of his eyes.

Dix said harshly: 'I'm not crying over this baby. He got what he asked for, what all rats get in the end. Why should a double-crosser get a quarter of a million bucks while honest cops work for peanuts? The hell with him!'

Uniformed cops and plainclothes

detectives closed in on the fat woman, sniping shots at her, keeping her bottled up. The D.A. called:

'You can't make a getaway, Madame Popocopolis — you're completely surrounded. Better give yourself up.'

She snarled defiance, firing back. A shell whined past the D.A., made him swear and dive for the shadows. He waved his men on.

'Get her!'

Madame Popocopolis turned at bay. She knew she had no chance; with Chandos, Nugent and Snowy dead, she would go straight to the hot seat if the cops took her alive. The gun was hot in her fat hand, the magazine almost exhausted. Her shabby black dress was torn and blood ran down her wrinkled face; her double chins mumbled ceaselessly and the breeze whipped at her straggle of grey hair. A barrage of crossfire made her change position. The cops were closing in remorselessly, cornering her like a wild animal. She blazed back at them, retreating further into the shadow of a giant elm.

The moonlight was bright on gaunt white tombstones. Bracken crackled under heavy feet; she could hear them breathing, so close were they. Every shadow seemed to hold a hunter; they lurked behind trees and marble slabs, crept up on her from behind mounds of earth bedecked with faded flowers. Death was all around her, waiting to claim her. Fear rattled the teeth in her gaping mouth.

She saw Thad Belknap then; impatient to finish his son's murderer, he came out into the open, gun in hand, intent for the kill. Ghostly moonlight shone on his bald head, transforming him into a grim, relentless nemesis. His eyes glittered with the light of vengeance.

Madame Popocopolis aimed her gun and squeezed the trigger; it clicked home on an empty chamber. Her gun was useless; it was the end. Belknap sprang forward, saw her, fired. He kept his gun on the trigger, pumping lead into her fat bulk until his gun was empty; but, by then, it no longer mattered. The fat woman lay sprawled under the cold moon, riddled with bullets, her last breath wheezing out from sagging lips. She looked horribly old and incredibly evil as she sprawled lifeless on the grass between ancient tombstones, The dragnet had done its work; the killers of Roy Belknap had paid the penalty and the law could go home once more.

Thad Belknap turned away; his face was grey and dull and he seemed to have aged ten years in as many seconds. His son was revenged; it was all over. He no longer had anything to drive him on; his life was suddenly without meaning and he shrank within himself. A broken man, he stumbled away into the night, his millions meaning less than nothing to him now. Nothing could bring back his son . . .

A cop's voice sounded from the house: 'We've got the girl!'

Johnny Fortune cursed; some blockhead had found Ava and mistaken her for her sister. He raced for the house, to find Ava with Dix and Tim Wilson and a couple of uniformed men.

Johnny glared at Dix.

'Take your bloodhounds off that girl — she's nothing to do with it. It's her sister you wanted . . . and she's past anything you can do to her.'

He held Ava close, soothing her, explaining things to Dix and the D.A. Finally, he satisfied them that Ava was in the clear.

Dix smiled, and his thin face wore a gentle expression.

'Okay, Johnny, take it easy. You've cleared the girl — and yourself! At one time, I thought . . . but never mind that now.'

The D.A. said: 'Yeah, I guess we've got nothing on you, Fortune — but another time, come clean. I don't like bright boys who think they know all the answers.'

Johnny grinned.

'Forget it, Wilson. Maybe I didn't use my head over this affair — but then, I'm in love, and . . . well, what can you expect?'

He took Ava's hand and led her outside. Settled in the coupé, he drove away from the house on 59th Avenue. The streets of New York were strangely quiet after the hectic gunfight, and Johnny drove slowly through the moonlight. Ava nestled beside him; she had stopped trembling and her eyes were dry.

She said, in a low voice: 'Poor Gail. If — '

Johnny pressed her hand.

'Don't think about it, Ava. It's over, and can't be changed. And what happened to Gail wasn't your fault, so put that idea out of your head.'

He fumbled in his pocket, brought out an official-looking document.

'A special licence,' he said lightly. 'We're going to knock up a parson and get married — tonight. Then I'm going to take you away from here, somewhere you can forget all that's happened. I'm going to spend the rest of my life trying to make you happy.'

He pulled the car into the curb, stopped, and turned to look into her eyes. His mouth was suddenly dry.

'That is,' he said, 'if you'll have me. Ava, will you marry me?'

Johnny thought how beautiful she looked, with bronze hair draping her shoulders, carmined lips slightly parted and her wide brown eyes flecked with gold. She smiled faintly and nestled closer.

'Johnny,' she said softly, 'of course, I'll marry you!'

His arm went round her waist, drew her close. His mouth covered hers in a long, intense kiss. When they broke away, all the fear and pain had gone from her face. The gold flecks were dancing in her eyes and they seemed to say, over and over again:

'I love you!'

Johnny Fortune laughed softly and started the car.

A new life was beginning; the exciting trail of adventure and danger lay behind him; ahead, was — what?

Ava asked him what he was laughing at, but he only shook his head. You can't very well tell the girl you're going to marry that life with her may be more exciting than murder and crime, can you? At least, Johnny Fortune couldn't.

We do hope that you have enjoyed reading this large print book.

Did you know that all of our titles are available for purchase?

We publish a wide range of high quality large print books including:
Romances, Mysteries, Classics
General Fiction
Non Fiction and Westerns

Special interest titles available in large print are:
The Little Oxford Dictionary
Music Book, Song Book
Hymn Book, Service Book

Also available from us courtesy of Oxford University Press:
Young Readers' Dictionary
(large print edition)
Young Readers' Thesaurus
(large print edition)

For further information or a free brochure, please contact us at:
Ulverscroft Large Print Books Ltd.,
The Green, Bradgate Road, Anstey,
Leicester, LE7 7FU, England.
Tel: (00 44) **0116 236 4325**
Fax: (00 44) **0116 234 0205**

Other titles in the
Linford Mystery Library:

DR. MORELLE AND THE DOLL

Ernest Dudley

In a wild, bleak corner of the Kent Coast, a derelict harbour rots beneath the tides. There the Doll, a film-struck waif, and her lover, ex-film star Tod Hafferty, play their tragic, fated real-life roles. And sudden death strikes more than once — involving a local policeman . . . Then, as Dr. Morelle finds himself enmeshed in a net of sex and murder, Miss Frayle's anticipated quiet week-end results in her being involved in the climactic twist, which unmasks the real killer.

THE THIRTY-FIRST OF JUNE

John Russell Fearn

There were six people in millionaire Nick Clayton's limousine when it left a country house party to return to London: Clayton himself, and his girlfriend Bernice Forbes; Horace Dawlish, his imperturbable servant and driver; the unhappily married financier Harvey Brand and Lucy Brand; and the tragic socialite Betty Danvers. But neither the car, nor its six occupants, would ever arrive in London. Instead, just after midnight, the car travelled some thirty miles along the country road — and disappeared . . .

MAIMED

Lyn Jolley

Joanna Coles was driving her children to school, as she did every morning of term time. On this particular dreary December day, however, a decision was being made about her, a decision of which she knew nothing. Soon after Christmas, Joanna Coles would be a name known to millions. Her photograph would appear on the television and in every newspaper in the land. Unfortunately, Joanna would know nothing of her tragic fame . . .

BOOMERANG

Sydney J. Bounds

The happy camaraderie of the Porth-
cove Studios holiday hotel is shattered
by the arrival of the misanthropic
George Bullard. He goes out of his
way to annoy both staff and fellow
artist guests. So when Bullard is found
brutally murdered, everyone in the
hotel comes under suspicion as having
a motive to kill him. Then there is a
second murder ... The police are
baffled, and it falls to the unorthodox
lady detective Miss Isabel Eaton to
unmask the killer.

THE FROZEN LIMIT

John Russell Fearn

Defying the edict of the Medical Council, Dr. Robert Cranston, helped by Dr. Campbell, carries out an unauthorised medical experiment with a 'deep freeze' system of suspended animation. The volunteer is Claire Baxter, an attractive film stunt-girl. But when Claire undergoes deep freeze unconsciousness, the two doctors discover that they cannot restore the girl. She is barely alive. Despite every endeavour to revive the girl, nothing happens, and Cranston and Campbell find themselves charged with murder . . .